MW01280160

# California Schemin'

by

## Kate George

# Mainly Murder Press, LLC

PO Box 290586
Wethersfield, CT 06109-0586
www.mainlymurderpress.com

# Mainly Murder Press

Copy Editor: Paula Knudson
Executive Editor: Judith K. Ivie
Cover Concept: Kate George
Cover Designer: Karen A. Phillips

*All rights reserved*

Names, characters and incidents depicted in this book are products of the author's imagination or are used fictitiously. Any resemblance to actual events, organizations, or persons, living or dead, is entirely coincidental and beyond the intent of the author or the publisher.

No part of this book may be reproduced or transmitted in any form or by any means, electronic or mechanical, including photocopying, recording, or by any information storage and retrieval system, without permission in writing from the publisher.

Mainly Murder Press
www.mainlymurderpress.com

Copyright © 2011 by Kate George
ISBN 978-0-9827952-4-8

Published in the United States of America 2011

Mainly Murder Press
PO Box 290586
Wethersfield, CT 06109-0586

# Dedication

To Sara and Buffy, my catalysts for change.
To you I owe much love. Thanks for having my back.

## Acknowledgements

Many thanks to Lisa, Doris, and TNT for your invaluable edits and suggestions. Thanks also to Marly and Ryan for titles, names and always being willing to play! Couldn't do it without you folks. Well, maybe I could do it, but it wouldn't be nearly as good.

My apologies to the citizens of the foothill communities north of Sacramento for changing the character and landmarks of your towns to suit my needs.

# One

She was falling, plummeting toward the river. Her skirt billowed, then wrapped around her as she tumbled. I watched her through the viewfinder, an unnaturally pink anomaly in sharp focus against the grey background of the bridge. I'd never be able to look at that color again without feeling the horror of seeing a woman plunging from the Foresthill Bridge. Half my brain followed her descent with my camera while the other half was in a blind, screaming panic.

"No!" I tossed the camera into my camp chair and sprinted upriver.

The riverbank was rocky, areas of stone ledge mixed with large rocks, boulders and pebble beaches. My heart pounded as I slipped and teetered, skidding over the smooth surfaces, tripping over loose stones. I scanned the river as I ran, watching for a splash of pink. Twice I stopped myself from falling by steadying myself on rocks, and my hands were stinging. I sucked air and held the stitch that developed in my side as I made my way up stream. The fall appeared horrific. Could she have survived? *Please, let her be alive.*

I was forcing down panic when I saw her floating toward me on the current. She was face down in the water, the pink skirt dark and clinging to her legs. I waded waist deep into the water and grabbed the back of her shirt as she floated by, towing her out of the rapids into a calm shallows at the shore. I needed to get her face out of the water, but I knew I wasn't strong enough to lift her. Blood mingled with the blonde hair feathering around her head in the slow water. A fresh adrenaline rush flooded my brain, and I began to panic. I had to get her air and stop the bleeding.

Reaching across her body, I grabbed the shoulder of her sleeveless blouse. I was able to pull her body part way out of the water but the fabric slipped from my grasp, and she was face down again. I took a deep breath and tried to calm myself. *Use two hands, Bree,* I told myself, *you can do it if you use two hands.* Then it hit me that I might have better luck if tried to roll her from underneath. I slid my hand under her, feeling for her arm. I caught what felt like her elbow and tugged. She floated into me. I pushed up on her near shoulder as I used her arm to pull her underside up. The movement of her shoulder started her rotating, and she flipped.

I saw I needn't have bothered. A hole in her temple oozed blood into her hair. Drowning had been the least of her problems, and the best I could hope for now was to get her out of the water so she wouldn't float away. I lurched from the river and lost my breakfast in the trees lining the riverbank.

My name is Bella Bree MacGowan. I'm called Bree by my friends, and I'm not exactly a stranger to dead bodies. It hadn't even been six months since I found my boss dead. I'd come to California to recover from the experience, and here I was chasing down another emergency. I hoped I'd be able to pull her from the water. I'm only five foot six and don't have too much heft to me. Luckily, I'm strong. With brown hair and eyes I like to tell people I look like Rachael Ray without the benefit of a stylist.

My last dead body had thrown me for a loop, but it hadn't been nearly as bad as this. Maybe it was because I didn't actually see Vera die, but discovered her afterward, that I was able to keep my stomach under control. Somehow this was different. The fall combined with the bullet hole was more than I wanted to deal with. I looked over to where her blonde hair drifted on the water. The blood was still mixing with the river water. Had she already been dead when she fell? I glanced up to where she'd fallen and saw the glint of reflection off glass. Someone was watching.

A chill went down my spine, but I waded back into the water anyway and pulled her to the shore. I hefted a couple of rocks onto the woman's skirt. I didn't want her floating away when I went to call for help. The sun was warm, and I pulled off my soaking hoodie as I scrambled back to where I'd left my stuff. I pulled the cell from my pack and punched 911. Unlike in Vermont, I always had cell service in California. Even out here at the bottom of a canyon, I could see the cell tower on the rise above the bridge.

I finished the call and made my way back up the river to the body. I sat on a fallen tree where I could see her but didn't have to look at her. Closing her eyes crossed my mind, but the last time I had touched a dead body I'd ended up as the only suspect in a murder investigation. *Bree, you've already touched her, it wouldn't hurt to close her eyes. Yes. Yes it would. My fingerprints would be on her eyelids.*

*That's just creepy. Besides, I don't want to lose what's left of my lunch.*

It would have been peaceful by the river if it weren't for the body. I turned so I wouldn't see her staring at the sky, but I felt like she was staring at me. Feeling ghoulish and creeped out, I slid down the side of the fallen tree until I was sitting on the ground. I knew it was childish, but there it was. Not even dead people could look through trees.

I flipped open my phone again and dialed Meg. Meg had been my friend forever and my boss for slightly less than that. The three-hour difference between Vermont and California worked in my favor. If I knew Meg, she would have been at work for a couple of hours already.

"I did it again," I said, trying to keep my voice steady and failing miserably.

"Well, hello to you, too. What did you do again?"

"Found a dead body."

"Oh, no, Bree. Not another one. Are you okay?"

"I threw up."

"Poor baby. What happened?"

"There's this really high bridge here, a thousand feet or something like that. I saw a woman fall."

"Wait. Where were you?"

"I was on the river bank taking pictures. I thought maybe the river was deep enough that she could survive the fall, but she'd been shot."

"Bree, wait. I'm lost here. Start over from the beginning. Like what you had for breakfast."

I took a breath, let the feel of the sun and the sound of the river help calm me. Then I told Meg that I had two eggs over easy for breakfast. And coffee.

Halfway through my narration I was interrupted by crashing in the undergrowth. I was wishing it could have been the sheriff, but it was too soon and coming from the wrong direction. The trail head was a good five minutes downstream from where I sat.

I got to my feet, panicked. A wild animal or murderer, I didn't want to see either one. I shoved my cell phone into my pocket without bothering to close it, ran for the nearest Ponderosa Pine and jumped to grab a branch. My hands stung, but I dragged myself up as quietly as I could and climbed as high as I dared while trying to listen and watch to see what was coming.

A bear ambled onto the rocks near the river. Wild animal, not murderer, but what if it mauled the body? Jumping down didn't seem like a wise idea, and I didn't have anything to throw at the creature. I pulled my phone from my pocket. Miraculously, Meg was still there.

"What is going on? You scared the bejesus out of me. All that running and crashing around."

"A bear," I panted. "A dang bear came out of the woods. I'm afraid it'll maul the body. What should I do if it goes for the body?"

"Where are you now?" The stress levels in Meg's voice were ramping up.

"Up a tree. I climbed it when the crashing around started. That's what you heard."

"Let me get this straight. You are up a tree, talking to me on the phone?"

"Well, if you're going to put it like that, yes. I'm sitting in a tree talking to you on the phone while a bear rambles around deciding if it wants to maul a dead body. But hey, what else could happen?" Oh, man, as soon as the words were out I knew I was jinxing myself. "Don't answer that. I'm going to yell at the bear and see if I can get it to go away. I'll call you back."

Meg called my name, but I'd already snapped the phone shut by the time it registered in my brain. The bear was sniffing the ground, not doing much of anything. I couldn't tell if it was a boy bear or a girl bear. I was hoping boy, because if it was a momma bear, I could be in real trouble. The jinx kicked in, and before I could start making a lot of noise to startle it, a man came crashing into the clearing.

He was clearly not a country boy. His shoes were black and shiny. He wore a suit. The only signs that he was aware of the lack of cement were the tie hanging out of his pocket and the top two buttons on his dress shirt, which were undone. He seemed unaware of the bear, his attention riveted by the blond lying in the water. I opened my mouth to warn him but he pulled a gun out of a shoulder harness. Of course I'd missed *that* in my initial assessment, and my mouth snapped shut. As much as I didn't want to watch anyone get mauled by a bear, I didn't want to end up dead even more. If this was the guy who killed the blond, then there wasn't much keeping him from killing me.

I was having a holy-crap-what-am-I-going-to-do moment when the cops showed. City boy ducked into the woods and took off running, which startled the bear. He saw the cops and ran splashing up the river. A fifty-ish Placer County Sheriff with a military style brush cut that was thinning on top appeared in time to watch the bear take his leave. The cop was on the heavy side, breathing hard from the hike. Behind him came two crime scene guys, significantly younger and more attractive. They headed straight for the body and started unpacking their bags of paraphernalia.

I dropped out of the tree, the phone rang, and the older guy made straight for me. I was uncertain what to do. If I went for the phone, he might misunderstand my intentions and shoot me. So I raised my hands in front of me so he could see they were empty.

"Aren't you going to answer that?" he asked me.

"Oh, sure." I yanked the phone from my pocket and flipped it open. "Meg, I've got to call you back. The sheriff is here. Give me a break, I'm fine. It'll wait."

I turned back to the Sheriff, knowing I was going to sound like a nut job. "Before you got here there was a man. A guy in a suit. He came out of the woods and went straight for the body. He heard you coming up the trail before you could see him, and he took off through there." I raised a hand to indicate where the guy had gone.

With a flick of the wrist he sent one of his crime scene guys after the suit. I heard him crashing around in the undergrowth for a while, but before long he was back. He shrugged at his boss and joined the other crime scene tech at the edge of the river.

"I take it you are the young lady who found the body? What in God's name were you doing up a tree?" He squatted in front of me and pulled his ID, a small notebook and a chewed pencil from his pocket. "Sheriff Lawrence Fogel. Most people call me Larry."

"I was up the tree because of the bear. Didn't you see it?" I pointed to where the bear was still visible, standing in the water upriver.

He looked and noted the bear on his pad.

"You have blood on your hands. You touch the body?"

I looked down at my hands. I hadn't realized they were bleeding.

"I grabbed her shirt and her arm, but it's not her blood. I scraped my hands on the rocks running up the river."

"And you were running up the river why?"

I nodded to where the two officers were now examining the body.

"I saw her fall from the bridge through my camera," I said. In my head I was thinking, *young lady? Who does he think he's kidding?* "I ran upstream to see if I could help her, but she'd been shot in the head."

"Probably dead before she hit the water." He scratched at the thinning hair on his head. "The question is, was she dead before she left the bridge."

"She was still bleeding when I pulled her to shore."

"Let's back up here. Why don't you tell me exactly what you saw? Start with …"

"I know, what I had for breakfast." I hadn't meant to cut him off, but it was out of my mouth before I could control it.

"Not quite that far back. How about your name and why you're up here today."

"Bella Bree MacGowan. People call me Bree. I'm here, well, in California, because my boyfriend is doing some masonry work. He asked me to come, which is nice, except there isn't much for me to do. I've been taking photos of the area to keep from going stir crazy. That's what I was doing today."

A cool breeze rippled down the canyon as afternoon turned to evening. Shadows crept up the sides of the canyon walls on the east side of the river. The air smelled clean, sweet even, but I was still damp from being in the river. I shivered.

"We came here a couple of weeks ago, and I thought I'd come back and take some pictures. I was shooting birds when a bright spot on the bridge caught my eye."

"Wait," Sheriff Fogel broke in. "You were taking pictures? Where's your camera now?"

"Down the river. You must have passed it; my stuff is near the trail head."

"Come with me. We'll go retrieve it. Digital or film?" he asked as we walked.

"Digital."

He led me down the trail and stopped at the flat spot where I'd left my stuff. I picked up my camera and clicked it on. I set the LCD display to review and handed him the camera. Fogel stepped into the shade so he could see the screen better, and I stood behind him so I could see what he was looking at. I'd taken the pictures, but I didn't know just what I'd captured. He flipped through photos until he got to the bridge shots.

The images were too small and too far away for me to be able to see any detail, but I had snapped the crucial moment when she began her plummet from the bridge and several shots of the fall. I didn't even remember my finger being on the button.

"Gather up your stuff. I want to get you out of here."

Sheriff Fogel walked me down to the road before they brought the body down. He ejected my memory card and put it in his pocket and handed me my camera. I stowed my pack and camp chair in the rear seat and tried to keep the images of the dead woman out of my mind.

Sheriff Fogel put his hand on my arm as I went to get in the driver's seat.

"Is there anyone at home?" His blue eyes scanned my face. Looking for a lie?

"My boyfriend should be home soon." I pulled my phone out of my damp jeans pocket and flipped it open to see the time. "Probably before I get there anyway."

"It'll be better for you if you aren't alone. Dead bodies have a way of preying on people's minds." He patted my shoulder and I wondered if he had a daughter of his own.

I didn't tell him this wasn't my first body and I knew the drill. If events followed the previous pattern, I figured I'd start shaking half way home and have to pull over for a while. Then I'd be fine.

Beau was sitting on the rustic porch swing when I drove up. We were living in a log cabin in the woods up Highway 49 north of Auburn. It had a covered porch across the front with a porch swing and flower baskets hanging from the ceiling beams. The other three sides of the cabin were surrounded by deck. The logs had been treated so they wouldn't weather with age, and it was a beautiful light red wood. I liked the windows best. They graced almost every vacant wall.

I climbed the steps and sat beside Beau on the swing. He dropped his arm around my shoulder and tugged me to him.

"Bad day?"

"Only if you count watching a woman fall a thousand feet from a bridge. I pulled her out of the water, but she had a bullet hole in her head. I couldn't save her."

"Oh, Babe. Come here." He wrapped his arms around me, and I leaned into him. His chest was like a warm and yielding brick wall. He didn't smell bad either. I leaned back and looked up at him.

"You must have been home a while. You smell like soap."

"Jumped in the shower. Figured I might as a well get cleaned up before you got home. He ran his hand across my cheek. "You okay?"

"I'm fine. I thought I could help, you know. I didn't know she'd be shot."

"That's a big drop, water's kind of shallow. I doubt she could have survived it." He slid his arm off my shoulders and got up. "Come on. I'm making dinner." He held his hand out to me, and I let him lead me into the cabin.

Beau served me burgers at the burlwood table next to a window overlooking the deck along the back of the house. We could watch the wildlife while we ate, which normally made me happy, but today the woods seemed oppressive and made me miss the open fields of home.

"I did something exciting today," Beau said as he swallowed the last of his burger.

"What's that? Did you complete that spectacular fireplace you've been building?"

"Nope. Remember how I told you this cabin's up for sale?'

"Yeah." Unease started to gnaw at my belly. *Please don't tell me that you bought it.*

"I bought it."

"You bought it. To live in all the time?" My voice was low and flat. Somewhere in my head I knew I should be trying to drum up some enthusiasm, but it took a while for my internal sensor to kick in.

"Yeah, to live in all the time. There's plenty of work out here. I love the weather. No relatives, although I will miss Tom's kids. But they can come visit me here." He looked at me, and I knew dismay was registering on my face. "What? I'm asking you to live here with me, Bree. Stay and enjoy being a Californian."

"Beau, I don't want to be a Californian. I don't think you could get the Vermont out of me."

"I thought you'd be thrilled to get away. Think about it, Bree. Here you get a fresh start. No one knew you in kindergarten or saw you skinny-dipping in the river. It's all new."

"I like that everyone knows me. I like the people in our town."

"What about how they treated you when Vera was murdered? All those dirty looks and whispers behind your back. You want to go back to that?"

"Almost everyone apologized." I looked down at the food left on the plate. The burger had lost its appeal, and the fries were cold. I dipped my fork in the pool of dressing I had on my plate and stabbed a few lettuce leaves. I looked at my laden fork for a moment and set it back down. My appetite had disappeared.

"Beau, I love that you brought me to California, but we've already been here two weeks longer than you said we would be. I'm writing articles and interviewing people long distance. Somehow it doesn't seem fair to Meg that I took on the job of staff reporter and then skipped town. And I'm missing my animals a lot. I want to go home."

"Why am I so surprised by this? You've always been a homebody. I guess somehow I thought that my being here would be enough to get you to stay. Shit."

I got up from the table and walked out onto the deck. The sun was dropping over the mountains, and the air felt cool on my skin. Somehow I'd had the impression California was warm all the time. Maybe San Diego was warm all the time, but the Sierra Foothills were cold in November.

I walked to the railing and looked into the woods surrounding the clearing we called our yard. Birds and small animals were hanging out in the trees. Sometimes at this time of day deer would wander across the clearing and munch on the flowers.

I liked Beau. A lot. Enough to leave my whole life behind? Probably not. It was so dang unlikely that we'd actually last. I didn't have the best track record with relationships. Things inevitably went wrong. I didn't want to be three thousand miles away from home when that happened.

I heard the sliding door open, and Beau came to stand beside me at the rail.

"I should have asked you first, shouldn't I?" He slid his arm across my shoulder and pulled me to him.

"I don't know. Probably wouldn't have made any difference. You would have bought the cabin anyway, and I would have eventually gone home. The outcome's the same." I rested my head on his shoulder. "So. What are you going to do with your house in South Royalton?"

"I'll keep it. I'll have my own space when I go back to visit. I'll get old Jamison to keep an eye on it for me." Beau paused for a moment. "What if we shipped Lucky and the dogs out here?"

"I don't know. Let me think about it." I knew in my heart the answer was no but didn't want to disappoint him. "I'm not sure I'm the California type."

"Bree, there isn't a mold that would hold you." One bark of laughter escaped him. "You are completely unique. I'm pretty sure you could adapt to any place you wanted to."

I smiled at him, thinking he'd put me in a difficult position. If I didn't stay, it meant I didn't want to try. At least to him.

"Stop looking so gloomy." He took my right hand in both of his, turned it palm up and examined the abrasions. "It's not as bad as all that. I bet I can make you forget all about today."

"I bet you can." I smiled up at him. Then a memory struck. "Do you know that the last guy who said that to me broke up with me just a few days later?"

"That dickhead, Jim?" Beau laughed. "You were better off without him. Come on. I bet I can make you forget better than he could."

"I bet you can."

He bent and kissed me. My fingers curled into his shirt as he wrapped his arms around my waist and held me to him. He broke off the kiss, and I took a quick step back to keep from falling over. He took my hand and led me toward the house.

"Come on, Sweet Cakes, I got something to show you."

I laughed.

"Something new? I'm pretty sure I've seen it all before." I grinned up at him as he slid the sliding door closed.

He slid his hand under my chin and kissed me lightly.

"You know I can't resist a challenge."

"I know." I broke free and ran down the hall, hearing his footfalls behind me. He caught me in a heartbeat, and all thoughts of the day were forgotten.

The next day I had an email from Sheriff Fogel: *Ms. MacGowan, it may be quite a while before we are able to return your photo disk, but I thought you would appreciate having the pictures that were on it. I'm not able to send the photos that are pertinent to our case, but the others are attached.*

I scrolled through the photos and noticed he'd made a mistake. There were two photos of the bridge before the woman fell. She was visible as a bright pink spot. I squinted. A bright pink spot flanked by a couple of dark figures. *I should enlarge these. Are you out of your mind? The less you know, the better.*

I shut down my laptop and stashed it under the bed. I felt kind of silly, but those pictures bothered me. I could have deleted them, but nothing is ever truly deleted. At least that's what I'm told. I'm only tech savvy enough to be dangerous.

Beau had one of his crew take him to work in the morning so I could have the car. I drove into town to pick up chips and beer. The road into Auburn was beautiful, and the weather was perfect for driving, so instead of stopping at the store I kept going down Highway 49 past the grocery, merged west on I-80, and headed toward Sacramento. Past Auburn the valley flattens and the highway widens as the farmland gives way to residential subdivisions, industrial buildings and shopping centers. The closer I got to Sacramento, the more congested the freeway became. Cities are not my favorite places. I'm used to open space and sparse population, but there was something I wanted to do. I took the off-ramp at Madison Boulevard, pulled into a shopping center, parked and made for the pet store. It was one of those cavernous box stores with rows and rows of pet supplies stacked to the ceiling. It was bright and antiseptic, except at the front where an area had been created with low ceilings and soft couches facing rows of glass fronted cages showcasing puppies. I sat on a red overstuffed sofa, asked the attendant to bring me a puppy and soaked in the affection.

Don't get me wrong. I don't have anything against men, but if you're looking for total devotion and unconditional love, go for a dog every time. Your dog will never ask you to move three thousand miles from home. In fact, your dog will follow you anywhere and be quite happy. They may resent you for leaving them in a kennel for a week, but they'll get over even that in a day or two. Guys are not quite so forgiving.

I spent an hour playing with puppies. They crawled on me, licked my face, attacked my fingers and slept in my lap. When the attendant finally whisked the last one away I felt much better. I still missed my dogs, but my heart felt lighter. I left the pet shop and zipped down the mall to the Safeway grocery store.

The drive home, while still an hour, seemed to fly by. I had the radio blasting and the windows open. I'd seen the Vermont weather on the internet, and they were in the midst of a "wintery mix." I did love being in the sunshine, at least temporarily.

The air conditioner was whipping my hair around as I turned up the one-lane road that led to Beau's cabin. Sometime during the day it had become Beau's in my mind. I wasn't surprised he'd bought it. The place suited him. The isolation, if anything, suited him more.

A quarter of a mile from the house I could see the commotion. There were a couple of cop cars and a pickup in the drive. Three officers were standing at the foot of the stairs talking to Beau, and a fourth was just coming out the door.

I parked on the side of the road, gathered up an armful of groceries and started up the drive. Beau and the cops noticed me, and the whole group headed in my direction.

"Here, let me take these." Beau took the groceries from me and set them in the bed of the pickup.

"There are more." I started back toward the car. I knew there had to be a good reason for the sheriff to be at the house, but I really didn't want to know what it was.

"Wait. Don't bring those up yet. I'm not sure we can go in." Beau glanced at the officer standing beside him.

I sighed and turned around. He was short-circuiting my efforts to ignore whatever crisis had befallen us now. I was supposed to be in California resting up from disaster. I wasn't all that keen on the fact that it had followed me here.

"Okay," I said, "lay it on me. What happened while I was gone?"

"Unfortunately," a brown-haired officer broke in, "the cabin door was forced, and it looks as though your husband's computer was stolen. The place was searched. Any idea what they were looking for?"

I let the husband label slide without comment, led them into the house and dragged my computer and camera out from under the bed.

"You'd better call Sheriff Fogel. I saw a woman fall off the Foresthill Bridge yesterday. They may have been looking for the camera I had with me. They must know that any pictures could have been downloaded. That's probably why they took Beau's computer. What they don't know is that I gave the photo disk to the Sheriff already. There isn't any point in stealing it from me."

The cops took off, leaving Beau and me to clean up the glass from the window that was smashed out of the door. Beau was quiet, and I didn't know what to say. Without meaning to I'd gotten back into trouble, and this time I'd dragged him in with me.

The house had been tossed. I put the cold stuff away but let the non-perishables wait. Whoever tossed the house either hadn't thought to look under the bed, or they hadn't gotten to it before they had to leave. Or maybe they thought they'd gotten what they needed when they nabbed Beau's computer. No, his computer was in plain sight. They wouldn't have had to search the house if they thought that was all they needed.

I went to stand with Beau, who had finished nailing a board over the broken window in the door.

"Do you think they'll come back?" I scanned his face for signs of stress. Life with Beau was generally easy. He was laid back, an affectionate and fun-loving guy. But strangers in his house was something out of his comfort zone.

"What makes you ask that?"

"They didn't find my camera or laptop. They don't know about my computer, but they could have seen my camera. I think that's what they were looking for."

"That depends on how badly they want to see those pictures. It's possible they'll try again. Tomorrow you're coming to work with me. I'm not taking any chances on them finding you alone." He wrapped his arms around me and kissed my forehead. "I don't care how determined they are, you are mine, and they can't have you."

"Better be careful, they'll be marking 'doesn't share well with others' on your report card." I was thinking that taking me to work was over the top, but I knew better than to try and argue with him when he was worried about me.

"Let 'em. I don't think sharing well with others was ever my strong point. Playing well with others, maybe, in the right circumstances. Come on," Beau smiled at me "I'm taking you into town for dinner.

The next morning as we were getting ready to leave, I rummaged around for a Sharpie and wrote a note on a piece of paper. It read: The Camera is at the Sheriff's Department. I taped it on the outside of the door.

Beau looked at my handy work and laughed. "They'll think you're bluffing."

"Well I'm taking both the camera and the computer with me, so tossing the house again isn't going to help them. I'm just trying to save us the trouble of cleaning up again. It's worth a try."

He put his arm around my shoulder and pulled me close to him as we walked to the truck.

"Did you hear the phone ring this morning?" he asked.

"Yeah, what was that all about?"

"I've got some bad news." He slid into the driver seat. "Michael likes what I've done so far, and he wants me to do some more stone work at the house. It'll be at least a couple more weeks before I'm done.

"How is that bad news?" I asked. I walked around and climbed into the truck.

"You told me yesterday you're ready to go home."

"Yeah, but you aren't. More work is a good thing." I hoped I was pulling off the appropriate empathetic tone, but my heart was sinking.

Beau smiled and dropped his hand on my thigh, so I guessed I was doing a good job with the whole supportive girlfriend thing.

The day passed peacefully. I sat in the sun reading and surfing the net while Beau pieced the stonework on the outside of the chimney. He packed up as the sun dropped behind the trees, and we headed into Nevada City for dinner and a movie.

We ate at Dave's Burgers and walked along the old-world streets lit with street lamps and twinkle lights to the theater. The three original *Star Wars* movies were playing. We bought candy and sat through one and two before I started to drift off.

"Bree," Beau whispered and shook my shoulder. "Let's get out of here before the next one starts."

"Okay." I stretched and gathered my coat and candy wrappers.

Out on the street Beau put his arm around my shoulder and pulled me close. We walked down the hill looking in shop windows.

"Such a pretty town," I said looking at the brick buildings and the lights. The windows were filled with paintings and funky clothes, candy and stuffed toys. "It's like Disneyland."

"Only better," said Beau. "We didn't have to pay to get in."

We turned into the dark side street where the truck was parked. Both passenger side tires were flat. We walked up the road. I was thinking we must have driven over a beer bottle.

"Shit," Beau said. "Someone broke into the truck."

We walked to the passenger door, and I noticed the window had been broken. I looked through the window and swore. The glove compartment had been forced open, and my camera was gone.

I checked under the seat. My computer was still there. I turned to Beau.

"They didn't find the computer, but why slash our tires?"

Beau shrugged. We were stranded until a tow truck could get us out of here. I was mad about losing my camera, but slashing the tires felt personal.

I dialed AAA on my cell, and we sat on a bench overlooking the river waiting for them to arrive. After sitting for an hour, a Nevada County cruiser pulled in behind the truck. A Placer County cruiser drove up a second later and parked behind the first sheriff. Fogel got out of the second vehicle and walked down to where we sat.

"Heard you're getting a little unwelcome attention." He looked up at the truck. "Anything missing?"

"My camera. That's all, except why did they have to slash the tires? Kind of mean."

"Probably just making sure you couldn't follow them if you showed while they were doing a B&E on your truck. Nothing personal."

"Seems like a warning to me." Beau scowled at Fogel. "Warning us to stay out of it."

"It feels personal to me. I liked that camera," I said.

"Did you see anything?" Fogel asked.

"Nope. We were out to dinner."

"Why didn't you take your camera with you?" He wasn't looking at me like I was dumb, so much. More like I was an alien with four eyes or something.

"Didn't occur to me that they would look for us here."

Fogel nodded. "I hate to say this, but I have to. You need to be more careful. House got busted into, tires got slashed. Sooner or later they may decide they need to talk to you, and the minute you see someone's face, you'll be a liability to them. They take killing women in stride."

"Did you find out who she is?"

"Not yet. I probably wouldn't tell you if I did know. You know too much already. I don't have the manpower to keep an eye on you and find the killer, too, so stay out of trouble." He went over to talk to the Nevada County Sheriff who was making notes.

"Yes, boss." I felt like sticking out my tongue or rolling my eyes at him, but I didn't. The fact that we had two slashed tires was a little too disturbing to make fun of the idea that I was in danger.

A flatbed tow truck came, replaced the flats with a couple of those little donut tires and loaded the truck. He took us to the twenty-four-hour service station which thankfully was also a tire shop. He dumped the truck and took my AAA information before he disappeared. By the time the shop replaced the tires and took my money, it was late. Beau was starving again, so we hit a drive-through and went home.

Beau parked, got out and sat down on the porch steps, looking up into the star filled sky. "You know this means they followed you, don't you? Someone is watching you."

"Well, they could have been driving by and recognized the truck." I didn't believe that for a minute. I knew they had to be watching. I was all bravado, bolstering myself up so I wouldn't look scared.

"Bree, I'm sending you home. You witnessed a murder, our home was burgled, and now they're following you. Who knows what they'll find on the camera? What if they enlarge one of those photos and see something? I don't want you to be the next one over the bridge."

"I gave the disk to Fogel. I don't think there are any photos on there for them to find."

"Then they are going to want to ask you what you saw, or, God forbid, they'll decide they are safer with you permanently off the scene, as in six feet under, not across the country."

"What are you saying? I have no choice but to go home? What if I don't want to go home? What if they follow me home?" This was my problem. I wanted to go home until someone told me I had to go home, and then I didn't want to anymore. I don't like people telling me what to do.

"Here's what I'll do. I'll tell everyone you went home to Virginia. When they say, 'I thought it was Vermont,' I'll say, 'You must have heard it wrong. I'm from Vermont,

Bree's from Virginia.' That'll confuse things. I'll tell Tom what's happened, and he can keep an eye on you. And you have all those dogs; they'll alert you if anyone strange shows up."

He stood up and took my hand.

"Come on. Let's get you packed."

"Wait." I resisted the pull on my hand. "What if my leaving puts you in danger? What if they come after you instead?"

"I'll be fine. There's no reason for anyone to come after me. I didn't see anything."

That's how I found myself lying in the back seat of the car, hiding from prying eyes, heading for the airport an hour before midnight.

"I'm not happy about this," I said. Beau was in the front seat driving.

"What?" He turned the radio down.

"I don't like this. I feel like a fugitive." I pushed off the blanket he'd thrown over me and sat up.

"You are a fugitive. Lie back down, for God's sake. Fogel said it was a good idea to hide you." He turned the radio back up.

"He didn't say I had to stay hidden all the way to the airport." I shouted over the radio. "We're on the freeway now, and nobody followed us out of town."

He turned the radio down midway through my sentence.

"You don't have to shout. I can hear you perfectly well. And just because I didn't see anybody doesn't mean there wasn't anyone."

"I was only shouting because you had the radio turned up. It's dark, Beau, how could anyone tell I was in here if they were following us?"

"They could see the shape of your head and surmise that you're in here. So lie back down."

"How about if I just slide down so my head isn't visible."

"Whatever, Bree. I'm tired of arguing with you." Then under his breath "It's not like I'm trying to save your life or anything."

# Two

We pulled into the short-term parking structure across from the Sacramento International Airport and trotted across the elevated pedestrian walkway that spanned Airport Boulevard. We had checked me in on-line and planned to get here at the last minute to reduce my visibility. Now we had to hurry.

I started toward the security checkpoint, but Beau took my arm and led me to the express line for employees and first class passengers. The passengers standing in the regular security line looked at us with curiosity. A few had open hostility on their faces. Standing in line has a way of bringing out the worst in people.

"What are we doing?" I asked.

"The Sheriff's Department got me permission to escort you to the gate. I'm not letting you out of my sight until you are on the plane."

"You don't actually think they'll try and pick me off at the airport, do you?"

"There's no point in taking chances. I can't imagine what Tom and Meg would say if something happened to you. I'm not going to risk being on the receiving end of Meg's wrath. No, I'm sending you back to where half the state police barracks is watching out for you."

"Only half?" I was inwardly rolling my eyes and trying to act naturally as TSA riffled through my purse and pulled out a tube of toothpaste and a bottle of moisturizer. I took them from him and handed them to Beau.

"Mail these to me, would you? That moisturizer is worth a fortune."

"That's because the other half is resting up from the stress of keeping an eye on you. I'm sure after you got stabbed in the arm by Dotty Post they upped the Bree alert by a factor of at least ten." He looked at the toiletries in his hand. "What do you want me to do with these?"

"Put them in your pocket and stop making fun of me. How many times do you think I'll find my boss dead? It's not likely to happen again." I hoped.

"How can you say it's a freak incident when you've already found another dead body? Why I thought California would be safe for you, I'll never know."

We cleared the checkpoint, pulled my carry-on off the conveyor, and he pulled me aside.

"Remember, when you get to Virginia you need to leave the airport in a taxi. Do you remember where to have him drop you? Did you bring money for the Metro?"

"Yeah, I remember. I'm not twelve you know. I can keep instructions in my head for longer than an hour." I knew he was worried and trying to protect me, but I was getting annoyed. The elaborate ruse of sending me to Virginia seemed like a waste of time. I knew from experience that paranoid people do strange things to protect themselves, but give them credit. If the sheriff was letting me leave the state, then it stood to reason that I didn't have any information. Beau was over-reacting, and the sheriff was going along for the ride. Or maybe it was the other way around.

My flight was announced over the PA, and we hurried toward the gate. My carry-on tipped off its rollers, and I dragged it behind me. Beau looked back and rolled his eyes. He took it from me, collapsed the handle and carried it the rest of the way. We reached the gate, and Beau set my case on the floor, grabbed the open front of my jacket and pulled me to him. The kiss he gave me about stopped my heart. The kind of kiss that shuts down brain function.

"What was that for?" I asked as he released me. My face was hot and I felt like I should be checking to make sure I still had all my clothes on.

"Making sure you don't forget me between here and Virginia. Now get on the plane. I'll be waiting here until it takes off." He kissed me again, this time on the top of the head and sent me down the jet way. Halfway down I remembered my toothpaste and ran back.

"I need my toothpaste and moisturizer."

"What?"

"My stuff." I rummaged in his pocket for the bottle and tube. "Where are they?"

"I left them at the check point. The officer said he'd hold them for me."

"Damn. I need them. I'm not going to do anything bad with them; I just forgot to put them in my suitcase."

"I'll mail them to you. Get on the plane."

"Jeez, when did you get to be so hard line?" I was still trying to work out how to get him to let me have my stuff back. "I don't want to have to buy that stuff in DC."

"And here I thought you were jogging back up the jet way because you already missed me." He planted another kiss on my head. "Go."

I dragged my bag onto the plane, wishing I could stay or that Beau was coming with me and wondering if this was really necessary. I settled into my seat. A small red-haired woman with clear blue eyes sat next to me, smiling tentatively. I smiled back, thinking she looked like a pleasant traveling companion, but I fell asleep after take-off and never found out.

I woke up briefly when we stopped to take on passengers in Las Vegas but fell asleep again when we took off for Virginia.

I woke as the plane landed and my usual disembarking debate started in my head. I thought the smart thing was to stay in my seat until everyone else got off. The other option was to stand up and be squeezed out like toothpaste. I decided I could be calm and wait, but when the plane stopped and the air stopped flowing, I started to get hot. I sat taking deep breaths, waiting for the doors to open. The cabin started to close in on me, and the air seemed hot. I was pretty sure they were filtering the oxygen out of it. I shot a look at the red head in the aisle seat, but she seemed calm. She certainly wasn't shoving her way into the horde between the seats, which is what I wanted to do. I wondered if I'd get arrested if I climbed over the other passengers and clawed my way out of the door.

I managed to keep my impulses in check and emerged from the plane hoping for a blast of cool air to soothe my overheated synapses. Unfortunately, the airport was hot and damp. It was raining outside, and the combination of wet travelers and heated air was stifling. I mentally ran through my usual list of swear words and headed for baggage claim, but the bank of monitors announcing departures caught my eye, and I stopped dead. There was a flight to Manchester, New Hampshire, leaving in a little over an hour. I stood there looking at the screen, needing to head for home but afraid I'd mess everything up. Meg would be waiting for me in Burlington in the morning. Beau and Fogel would flay me alive if I didn't show up at the hotel, and there was no guarantee that I wouldn't be stranded in Manchester. All this subterfuge was annoying.

I dragged my luggage off the conveyor belt in baggage claim and wheeled it out to the taxi stand. I was about to get in a cab when I saw the hotel shuttle. I didn't actually like the idea of paying for a taxi ride to the underground and taking it to a stop three blocks from the hotel. Besides, it was really unnecessary, so I jumped on the shuttle.

An irrational feeling of relief washed over me when the driver unloaded my bag at the front of the hotel. Nothing bad had happened, and I hadn't been required to muscle my two-ton bag through the bowels of Washington. A bellhop practically ran through the rotating door and took charge of my luggage. I'd have to remember to stay in first class hotels more often.

I smiled at the desk clerk and handed him the business card that Sheriff Fogel had given me. The clerk immediately stood a little straighter. He began tapping furiously on the keyboard.

"Would you like an upper or lower floor, Ms. MacGowan?"

"Upper, I think, as close to the top as I can get." I was thinking a nice view would be good. Maybe I'd get lucky and get a view of the National Mall. Hah! More likely it would be an alley or a brick office building within arm's reach of my window.

"I have a penthouse suite on the top floor. The elevator has a special key so no one can come up without your permission. Would that be to your liking?"

"I don't really think that's necessary, and I'm not sure Fogel would want to pay for that, um, fancy a room." I wasn't supposed to say anything about who I was or who was paying, but this was ridiculous. A penthouse suite?

"The room is complimentary, madam. There is no need for you to worry. Is there anything else you will be needing? I can have meals sent to your room."

"That would be fine. Thank you."

He handed me a card key that operated the elevator and opened the room. The bellhop escorted me up in the gilt-lined lift to the top floor. What he must have been thinking I had no clue. The elevator doors were mirrored. My reflection showed tousled brown hair, rumpled T-shirt, faded jeans and my dirty black cowboy boots. I looked slightly disreputable and very rumpled after the flight, but they were treating me like some kind of dignitary. Or a fugitive.

I tipped the bellhop at the elevator after he dragged my suitcase into the hallway. Across from the elevators a set of shiny red doors framed with gold filigree faced me. I slid my card key through the electronic lock on the double doors. They opened into the suite, and I caught my breath. Floor-to-ceiling windows looked out over the city from three sides. From where I was standing I could see Washington through the open living area. History oozed from the city.

I dropped my suitcase and flung my purse onto the bed. I sank onto the couch and dug my cell out of my pocket. I didn't know who to call first, Meg, who would be awed, or Beau, who must know what Fogel had said to the hotel to get me such a fabulous room.

I called Beau first, just so I could get the scoop and tell Meg. It would be so much more satisfying if I could tell her the whole story.

"So," I said after I'd updated him on my flight, "what did I do to get the penthouse suite overlooking DC? I've got a special key to the elevator and everything." I flipped the key card in my hand thinking of possibilities.

"Fogel pulled some strings and got you in under witness protection. I don't know what he actually told the hotel, but from what I understand, they think you're either a visiting dignitary, an undercover agent, a fugitive from another country or a movie star with somebody stalking you. The truth never entered the picture. It's immaterial to the hotel. The chain gets paid to keep a certain number of rooms free across the country, and law enforcement can put anyone they want into them."

"So the guy that checked me in thinks I'm a spy?" This was too good to be true.

"Probably. Promise me you won't do anything foolish there."

"Won't even leave the room, most likely." *Well, probably, anyway.*

I would stay in the hotel. I felt safe in my tower with the outrageous view and room service. I took a shower. At first I was self conscious about the lack of curtains, then I figured anyone diligent enough to find a way to catch a glimpse into a penthouse bathroom when there was actually something to see deserved the reward.

After the shower I lay down on the bed, looking forward to flipping through channels and watching trash television. It was a guilty pleasure I almost never indulged in. Kind of hard to indulge with no TV in the bedroom and only three channels to boot. I discovered a Sudoku book in the drawer with the TV remote and looked to see how hard the puzzles were. The trouble with Sudoku is that it never fails to put me to sleep.

I woke up mid-afternoon, ordered a turkey sandwich from room service and flipped the flat screen back on. As the sun went down and the lights on the mall came on, the city became even more irresistible. I concentrated on the TV, trying to ignore the pull of the vista in front of me, but there wasn't anything remotely as interesting as the city below. I pulled myself together, swiped some mascara through my lashes, shrugged on a jacket and headed out to see the monuments.

Outside the hotel I thought for a minute about hailing a cab, or rather having the doorman hail me a cab while I waited in the warmth of the lobby, but how often was I going to get the chance to walk the Washington Mall? A woman was leaning against the brick wall of the hotel. She had stringy brown hair and wore a stained, camel-colored coat hugged to her body and ratty jeans. She pushed herself upright and approached me.

"I can give you a tour," she said. "Twenty-five dollars. I can show you everything you want to see."

"Are you a taxi driver?" I asked. There weren't any taxis parked nearby.

"No." She ducked her head. "You'd have to pay the taxi separate."

"Thanks for the offer, but I think I'll walk." I started across the street toward the expanse of the mall, the woman shadowing me.

"No, really, I'm set," I said as I stepped up onto the curb on the other side of the road. She was next to me matching me stride for stride. "Maybe some other time." But she stuck to me as I headed down the sidewalk. A knot was forming in my stomach, not that I thought I was really in any trouble, it was just odd. I was a weirdo magnet.

I looked around for a place where I wouldn't be alone and spotted a mounted police officer near the Washington Monument. I headed toward her. My shadow veered off as I went to pat the horse and chat with the officer.

I stood under the Washington Monument for a few minutes. The marble glowed in the flood light. It was huge, and I felt minuscule. The Lincoln Memorial glowed from the other end of the reflecting pool and I headed across the grass, down the mall away from the capital. The reflecting pool was long and I pulled my jacket around me and increased my speed. I didn't want to work up a sweat, but I wouldn't mind being just a bit warmer.

Like the Washington Monument, Lincoln was lit by floods. It glowed in the twilight. The lights had come up all along the mall from the capital to Lincoln and from the White House to Jefferson. It was almost magical. It would have been fabulous if I wasn't so dang cold and more than a little freaked out.

As I mounted the steps to get a better look at Abe, I saw movement. There was a woman standing in the rotunda reading the writing on the wall. She was smartly dressed, plaid skirt and a short black pea coat. Sensible shoes. She glanced over and gave me a shy smile before turning her gaze back to the script. She seemed more nervous about me than I was about her, so I relaxed and turned to Lincoln.

He was imposing up there on his throne. Well, I guess it was really a chair, but he was kind of like a king sitting up there surveying the mall. Like an Egyptian prince or something. I turned to read the words engraved on the wall but I got the uneasy feeling that the woman was watching me. Normally, I would have pushed the feeling aside, but I chickened out and headed back down the steps and onto the mall.

The Vietnam Memorial was more imposing than I had expected it to be. I ran my hand along the names and let sorrow wash over me. Tens of thousands of lives cut short. Was there a name here that was related to me in some way? There were so many of them. I walked down the wall still trailing my fingers along the stone and noticed the woman from the Lincoln Memorial standing in the shadows. She shouldn't have surprised me, since we were both touring monuments. But the uneasiness returned, and besides, I was cold. I turned and headed back to Pennsylvania Avenue.

The hotel clerk winked at me as I passed through the lobby. I bet he didn't wink at the senators like that. *It's because he thinks I'm some kind of spy.* I keyed myself up the elevator and into my room. The joy had gone out of the day, not that it had been all that great to begin with. I missed Beau. I set the alarm so I didn't miss my flight and crawled into bed.

I made the airport in good time the next morning and didn't have any trouble with security, as Beau had my cosmetics in his pocket. I made a mental note to call and remind him to mail the stuff to me, otherwise they'd still be in his pocket next time I saw him. I was one of the first people seated on the plane. I took a window seat toward the front and concentrated all my energy on looking like an unfriendly seat hog in hopes of not being crammed in with two other people all the way to Burlington.

My scowl seemed to be working well until a very plump woman with shocking pink hair squeezed herself into the aisle seat. At least no one was likely to try and sit between us. I rested my head on the window and hoped I'd be able to concentrate on my book for the flight home. I sometimes got the willies on airplanes. My legs would twitch, and I wouldn't be able to sit still or concentrate. I dreaded flights like that.

"I wanted to warn you," the pink-haired woman leaned over to me. "I sometimes have trouble controlling my shape-shifting at high altitudes. Don't be alarmed if my hair changes color or my nose changes shape, okay?"

"Uh, okay," I said. My luck, I'd gotten stuck with a loony. "How long have you been a shape shifter?"

"Oh, my whole life. I'm from another planet. It's pretty normal there."

Correction: I was stuck with an alien loony.

I focused on my book and had a good start on it when the alien shape shifter got up to use the rest room. I caught myself wondering if she could fit in the tiny airplane toilet and felt bad. Wasn't fat one of the last acceptable prejudices? I should know better. I was mentally berating myself when she came back. I tried not to stare, but I could swear she was thinner, and her hair, while still pink, was several inches shorter.

She caught my look and smiled.

"I warned you," she said. "I know it's a bit startling if you aren't used to it. I'm lucky I my hair didn't go green or something. That's happened before."

"Why does this happen in airplanes?" I couldn't believe I was calmly chatting about the problems of a shape shifter.

"Something about the change in pressure? I'm not sure myself. I'm not the only one to have trouble at high altitudes. Others have this problem too. It causes a lot of trouble, believe me."

"What's your name?"

"You can call me Madison. My alien name is unacceptable in English."

"Can you say it for me?" This was getting curiouser and curiouser.

"All right, but I'm warning you, it's rude."

"No worries. I'm not easily offended."

She whispered something.

"I'm sorry, I couldn't hear that."

"Fuckwitz," she said. "It's Madassa Fuckwitz. I told you it was rude."

I used all my self control and didn't burst into laughter, but I made a mental note to have a howl with Meg over Madassa Fuckwitz when I got home.

I didn't comment when a while later Madassa "Madison" Fuckwitz disappeared into the bathroom and came back fifty pounds lighter and blue haired. I'd been warned.

By the end of the flight Madison was four inches taller and a hundred pounds lighter than when she got on the plane. Her hair was back to pink, but now it was the color of cotton candy and was cut in a smart little bob. I saw the stewardess give her a puzzled look as we exited the plane.

"Shape shifting alien," I said as the flight attendant smiled and said goodbye.

"What?"

I inclined my head in the direction of MMF.

"She's a shape shifting alien, that's why you don't recognize her. She has trouble maintaining her appearance during flights."

The attendant was looking at me as though I'd grown a second head. I smiled and got off the plane. *Are you losing your mind, Bree? You don't honestly believe in aliens, but you just made an ass out of yourself anyway.*

Meg was waiting outside the security check area with Gemma and Louise, as always. Meg was a little shorter and a little heavier than me. The girls both had their mom's curly brown hair, and twelve-year-old Louise had her eyes. Gemma's brilliant green eyes weren't inherited from anyone, as far as Meg could tell. If you asked Gemma, she'd tell you she was a changeling.

The girls squealed when they saw me and darted through the line of passengers to get to me. They almost flattened a little man who was foolish enough to cut between us when I stopped to brace myself for impact. Their little arms twined around me as they blurted out all the important news.

"Bree! We thought you were never coming home." "Annie hasn't eated anything since you've been gone." "Did you know that Rosie is pregnant?" "Annabelle pooped on your bed, but momma cleaned it up."

They towed me along, peppering me with questions and filling me in on the day-to-day progress of my animals. Meg smiled at me and shrugged. We'd say our hellos later when the girls calmed down.

"Where are the boys?" I managed to sneak a question in.

"Stayed home with their dad," said Meg.

"The boys couldn't be bothered to ride in the car for so long," said Louise.

"They wanted to stay home and play horseshoes in the barn with daddy," said Gemma. "Bree, when is Uncle Beau coming home? We miss him."

"He'll be home in a couple of weeks, Hon." The fact that Beau was planning to stay in California skittered through my brain, making me uneasy. Tom, Meg's husband and Beau's brother, had every right to know what was up, but I wasn't about to spill the beans. Let Beau break their hearts. I wasn't about to.

Meg was oddly quiet on the drive home. Louise and Gemma filled the time with chatter about school and the goings on around town while I was away.

"We saw Jim yesterday, Bree." Louise was smiling. Jim Fisk was my newest ex-boyfriend. "He told Jeremy that he's not dating Lucy Howe, even though she is always hanging around him. He d said to make sure that you knew that he wasn't seeing anyone. Only Jeremy didn't come, so I get to tell you."

"That takes a lot of nerve, asking your kids to pass on that he's not dating. What a jerk."

"He likes you, he knows he made a mistake, and he's rightly scared to death of you. I think the kids just seemed like a safe option," said Meg. "Not that I think you should get back with him, because I don't. I'm just saying he's not a bad guy, just stupid."

"Point taken. How are things with you and Tom? Has he got the barracks under control and stopped working overtime so much?" Tom was the Captain in charge of the local Vermont State Police Barracks where overtime was a given. Even rural Vermont kept the State Troopers busy.

"Oh, he still works too much, but it's not as bad as before. And we've been going out once a week and leaving Jeremy in charge. He's doing okay with it, but the other kids," Meg nodded toward the girls in the back seat, "give him a hard time. We had to lay down some pretty strict rules to keep things from getting out of hand."

"Sounds like things are getting better."

Meg nodded.

"Yeah, pretty much. How are things with you and Beau? Is he still mad at you?"

"I don't think he was mad so much as worried. He thought if I came to California everything would be OK. I'd be safe and he wouldn't have to worry about crazed soap stars or murderous housekeepers. I can't say as I blame him. I thought finding dead people was a one-time thing myself."

I looked out over the landscape. So different from the dry and warm California hills. There was a layer of snow over the countryside, smoke was rising from chimneys, and Christmas lights were already glowing along farmhouse eaves. It would be cold, grey and muddy until the world froze solid in January. Watering my animals would be a struggle until spring. I felt a smile spreading across my face. I was home.

A sea of dogs jumped on the car as we drove into the farm at Windstorm Valley. It was a big rambling farmhouse, painted white with black shutters. Meg's dogs, my dogs, and Beau's Chihuahua surged around us on the porch, Beans jumping higher and squeaking as loud as he could to make himself noticed in the pack.

Beau wasn't really a Chihuahua kind of guy. Jim had attempted to bribe me with Beans, but being high-minded and damn smart, I refused him. Beau took the baby in because he knew I hated to see the puppy go back to the breeder. In a way, Beans was mine, too, although I never once said it out loud. The minute I did that Beans would be living with me full time.

I ate lunch with Meg's family and then loaded the dogs in the car and headed up the hill towards home. It was difficult driving. My dogs had missed me and were taking turns trying to slide under the steering wheel into my lap. I compromised by driving with my left hand and rubbing ears with my right. When I unloaded them they were so overjoyed by the smells of home that they left me completely alone.

My house is smaller than Meg's and has more than the normal number of windows. I'd inherited the farm from my Grandmother. The little money I had inherited with it I put into windows and insulation so that the house was warm and full of light. It was painted the same yellow it had been when my Gram had lived there, with lots of charcoal grey shutters that I'd added with the windows.

I stepped up onto the porch, through the glass paned door into the kitchen and was overwhelmed by the smell of cat litter. Jeremy was supposed to be taking care of Annabelle, but apparently he hadn't taken his responsibilities too seriously. Granted, there was lots of food and water, but the state of the cat box was dismal. I dumped the contents of the box into a trash bag and took both the bag and the box outside. The dirty litter I happily dumped into the trash. The box I took over to the barn and rinsed it out in the big porcelain sink in the tack room. The sink drained via hose onto the ground at the rear of the barn, so I didn't have to worry about the litter clogging the septic. The thing smelled much better after a good cleaning, and I let it drip in the sink while I went to see my elderly pony.

Lucky turned his back the minute he saw me.

"Hey, buddy. I'm home."

I slid back the bolt and pushed open the door to his stall. He stood stubbornly with his head in the corner pretending to ignore me. I walked up to his rump and put a hand out to scratch above his tail, a tactic that had always worked in the past. A rear hoof whizzed past my leg, barely missing my knee. I grinned. I knew if he'd wanted to connect, he would have.

"Okay, I get it. You don't like it when I go away." I spoke quietly, working my fingers up his spine through his shaggy winter coat. "But I'm back now, and I'm sure Max took good care of you while I was gone." I went on talking nonsense and assuring him there was no better pony in the world until he relented and turned his head to me, resting his muzzle in my palm. I scratched between his eyes and around his ears. He puffed through his nose, giving me what I'd always thought of as a pony kiss, before I threw him some hay and went to check on the other animals.

All seemed right with the world in the barn. I closed up and took the cat box back to the house. I refilled the litter and went in search of Annabelle. I gave up when she didn't come to her name. She'd come out when she figured

I'd been adequately punished, but I kept an eye out for her as I climbed the stairs, thinking I could coax her out if I knew where she was.

The smell hit me half way down the hall to my room. Normally my room was my favorite spot in the house. It was filled with light and little else besides the bed and dresser. I looked through the open door with more than a little apprehension. I had a feeling I'd be sleeping in one of the other bedrooms tonight. Sure enough, the bed was covered with anything a cat could possibly deposit. Not only had she used it as a litter box, there were dead mice, hairballs and vomit littered over my beautiful blue and white quilt. A dead snake was gracing my pillow. At least I hoped it was dead.

# Three

I closed the door and walked away. Crap. Not what I'd wanted to come home to. I checked the rest of the rooms, but my bed was the only place where Annabelle had seen fit to notify me of her displeasure. I held my nose and went back in to open the windows. Then I went to the bed, used a wire hanger to remove the snake from the pillow and folded the whole mess up in the quilt.

I dragged the quilt downstairs and dumped the contents out behind the barn. Then I hung the quilt on the line, hoping that it would either rain or snow soon and wash some of the grossness away. If it didn't I'd wrap it in a plastic garbage bag and take it down to the laundry. If a couple of go rounds in the industrial washers didn't clean it up then I'd have to give the quilt up as a lost cause.

I was dragging my three-ton suitcase up the stairs when the phone rang. I left it on the landing and jogged back to the kitchen.

"You made it home safe." The sound of Beau's voice hit me in the stomach and made me long for him.

"Yeah, no problems. Did Fogel ever find out who it was I fished out of the river?" I hated the thought that she might remain anonymous, her family never knowing what happened to her.

"Yeah, but hang on, Fogel wants to tell you himself. I'll pass you over." There was some shuffling on the other end of the line. I leaned back and put my feet up on the kitchen chair next to me waiting for Fogel to get to the phone.

"The woman is Lily Carver Wallace, wife of R. Carl Wallace, member of the state senate." Fogel sounded distracted.

"Wow. How's he taking it?"

"Publicly devastated. Privately, not so much. Resigned I'd say, but not overly emotional."

"The wife of a state senator. That opens a can of worms, doesn't it? Is he liked? Not that it's any of my business."

"It's your business in that they chose to involve you. He's not well loved by a certain faction, but I fail to see what they could gain by killing his wife."

"Did the senator and his wife get along? They weren't in divorce proceedings or anything, were they?"

Fogel laughed. "You think like a cop," he said. "Again, publicly, everything was as it should be. Privately, I don't know. We've got people looking into it. The thing about it is, now that a senator is involved, the state police want to get involved. It's my jurisdiction, but I'm not sure I'll be able to hold on to this case."

"What will happen at my end if the case gets transferred? Will anybody be looking out for me, or am I on my own again?" I didn't like the sound of this. The last thing I needed was to end up involved in another murder investigation.

"I'll stay involved as much as I can, keep an eye on what's happening, but if I stick my nose too far into it, they'll politely ask me to mind my own business."

I sighed. On my own again. Not that I couldn't take care of myself; I could. I'd just rather not face a killer on my own.

"Would it be okay if I contacted my state police and tell them what happened? I'd feel better if someone local knew what was going on."

"Sure. Better still, give me the number, and I'll clue them in. Is there someone in particular I should contact?"

I gave him the name of the detective who investigated my boss's death and asked to talk to Beau. He called Beau to the phone, and I could hear more shuffling around.

"What's going on over there?" I asked. "Sounds very suspicious."

Beau laughed.

"Poker game in Fogel's kitchen. His wife won't let the guys smoke their cigars anywhere else. It's not a huge room, and there are about ten of us. Every time anybody has to use the phone, open the fridge or go to the john, we all have to shuffle around. You wouldn't believe it. And the phone is attached to the wall with a three foot cord. No leeway."

Jealousy crept over me. Here I was all alone, not counting four dogs and a very pissed off cat, and there he was in a room full of guys having a great time. The thought that they were probably hot and sweaty and really stinky didn't make me feel any better. I'd rather have a sweaty man in my bed than a dead snake.

I left the windows open in my room and slept in my mom's childhood room. It was comfortable enough, but I'd been looking forward to being back in my own bed. I lay in bed and sulked, but travel fatigue caught up with me, and I was asleep before I could really work myself up.

The next morning I woke to Annabelle on the pillow next to me. I thanked the powers that be that she hadn't brought a snake with her. We spent some time making up, me telling her how beautiful she was until she rolled over and let me rub her belly. I went downstairs, wolfed some toast and drove my Toyota All Trac down the hill to the newspaper office.

I parked in front of the laundry, took the stairs two at a time and opened the door into the sun-filled office. It was quiet and empty, too early for Meg or Deirdre to be in yet. I booted up my computer and rifled through the messages tucked under the keyboard. It was strange to be so happy to be at work, but it was good. I looked out onto the green, empty at this hour, with bare trees and brown grass. *You're back in your element, MacGowan.*

I got up, turned on the CD player and plugged in the coffee maker. I turned back to the computer and pulled out my notes. I was typing them up when footsteps on the stairs disturbed my concentration. I looked up from my computer when the door opened.

"MacGowan." Lieutenant Miles Brooks came through the door. "I understand you've got yourself mixed up in another murder. What did I tell you about staying out of trouble?"

"Hey, Miles! Haven't seen you in a while." I smiled at him. He had let me believe I was a murder suspect for a really long time in the autumn, but he'd made it up to me, and we had become friends.

"Yes, but isn't that a good thing?" He was smiling. "And as you aren't suspected of any crimes, I can ask you to coffee."

"You came up here to ask me to coffee? You could have just called."

He shook his head.

"I was contacted by Officer Fogel of the Placer County Sheriff's department and thought I'd drop in on you. Can I sit down for a minute?"

I nodded, and he pulled Meg's office chair across the floor to my desk. He sat across from me and stretched his legs out. He was as good looking as ever. Tall, blue eyed, dark haired and fit, he made the green and tan uniform look good. He scrutinized me over his fingertips

"Didn't you go to California to get away from trouble?"

"Why does everyone keep saying that? I didn't get into trouble. I did a good thing, pulling a woman from the river. I didn't know she'd been shot. Had I known that, I would have run in the other direction and never looked back."

"No, you wouldn't. If there was any chance she was still alive, you would have tried to save her. You wouldn't be able to help yourself."

"Nope. I'm getting smarter. I would have let her float down river until someone else discovered her."

"How you can lie like that without even twitching an eyelid is beyond me. I admire that quality in a cop, but you? Scares me."

"I am not lying! If I had known that trying to rescue that woman was going to make me a target, I would never have pulled her out of the water. Never. Anyway, if you were there you would have done the same thing."

"Maybe."

"Don't maybe me. You would have pulled her out even if you knew she was dead. Talk about lying."

Miles threw his head back and laughed. He pulled his legs back and sat up, leaning into me, his arms on my desk.

"But what are we going to do about you now? There seems to be some chance that this guy is going to come looking for you. How are we going to keep you safe out there in the woods by yourself?"

"I've got my dogs. Nobody in their right mind is going to tangle with four dogs." I pushed my keyboard back and leaned my elbows on my desk.

"There are ways to get around dogs, and you know it, but as there hasn't been any indication that anyone followed you home from California, I'm going to content myself with checking in on you. Daily. Okay?"

"Sure, if you don't have anything better to do with your time. No criminals on the loose at the moment? No dead bodies up at the Inn?"

"Nope. Nothing to do but keep my eye on wayward newspaper reporters. Come on, let's go downstairs and get some wicked good coffee."

"You do know I have a habit of dumping coffee on people, don't you?"

"I had heard a rumor along those lines. I'll risk it."

"How long are you intending to be in the office today?" Miles asked as we were clomping down the stairs. Well, I was clomping; he was descending the stairs with his usual measured pace.

"Just a little while longer. I promised Meg I'd come by for lunch. Why?"

"No reason."

I pushed through the lower door, stepped out onto the sidewalk and froze. Miles ran right into me and grabbed my arm to keep me from falling flat on my face.

"What's up?"

"I'll tell you inside. Come on." I led him into the coffee shop and slid into a booth near the front where we could see out the window.

"Did you see that woman out there?"

"I'm a cop. Of course I saw her. Why?"

"She sat next to me on the plane from DC. Claimed to be an alien shape shifter. Sure enough, she went from a short, heavy woman with bright pink hair to a tall, thin woman with cotton candy colored hair. I think even her eye color changed."

"All at once or in stages? Not that it really matters."

"Stages."

"So you'd make the connection. I'm less concerned about her shape shifting than I am about the fact she followed you from DC and probably from California before that. Stay here, I'm going to talk to her." Miles slid out of the booth and was out the door before I could collect my thoughts. He disappeared from view. Sandy brought the coffee and muffins, and I occupied myself with loading my muffin with butter.

By the time I got around to dumping the little plastic container of half-and-half into my coffee Miles was sliding back into his seat.

"What was that about?" I asked. I emptied a couple of packets of sugar into my coffee.

"I couldn't find her." He looked perplexed. "Went around the block looking in all the shops. Disappeared."

"Yeah, but why did you want to talk to her in the first place?"

"Are you kidding me? A strange woman follows you from California, where you just happened to see a murder, and I'm supposed to ignore her?"

"She seemed harmless enough." I watched Miles cut his muffin into four pieces.

"No such thing as coincidence. No such thing as harmless. Evidence, allegiance and circumstances … those things matter."

"You're such a cop. Don't you ever just forget about that stuff?"

"Nope, especially not when the circumstances revolve around someone I care about."

I looked to see if he was pulling my leg, but he was concentrating on buttering the four quarters of his muffin. I felt my cheeks getting warm, and I wondered if I should remind him about Beau. About the time I realized my mouth was hanging open he glanced up and saw me staring at him. I snapped my mouth shut but couldn't think of anything to say.

"I care about everyone in my jurisdiction, Bree." He was so matter of fact that I felt foolish for thinking differently.

"Oh, yeah, of course." Could I get any more lame? I took a sip of coffee and focused on not burning myself or spilling it when I set it down. Life took so much concentration sometimes, it exhausted me. I looked around and noticed Steve Leftsky, esteemed State Trooper and one of my lifelong friends, sitting at the back of the café.

"Hey, Steve's over there. Want to ask him to sit with us?"

Brooks turned and looked.

'Normally, I'd say yes, but he's been lousy company lately."

"How come?"

"Didn't you hear? Shirl dumped him. Said he was spending too much time at the barracks or hanging out at the bar with the guys." He shot me a sideways look. "Your name was also mentioned."

"You've got to be kidding me. She brought that up again? I've never even dated Steve. Never. Not even in high school. That girl's got something wrong with her brain."

Brooks shrugged, but I couldn't let it go, so when Miles headed back to work I went and sat with Steve.

"Hey," I said as I slid into the chair across from him. "What's up?"

"Nothing. Just taking a break."

"Anything new in your life?"

"You heard didn't you? Someone told you that Shirl left me. God, I wish people would mind their own business."

"Sorry." I stood up. "Thought you might like to talk about it. Give me a call when you feel like company."

I turned away, but he called me back.

"Oh, sit down! I wasn't talking about you; I was talking about whoever told you. Can't keep a damn thing a secret in this town."

"You expected that would change?"

"No, I'm just mad. I was trying to get a promotion at work, and you know how social it is. Who you know, not what you know."

I nodded. I did know.

"So I was hanging out with the guys, trying to be more of a team player so I could maybe get a raise. Shirl asked me to cut it out, and I said no, not until promotions were handed out. She kicked me out. Said she had to be more important than work or it was over. I'm bunking with one of the guys for now."

"Do you want me to talk to her? I might be able to get her to change her mind."

"Shit, no! You're part of the problem. She doesn't believe we're just friends. Thinks there has to be something going on. Just leave it alone, Bree. I'll figure it out. I'm thinking I may have to ask her to marry me. That might settle her down a little."

"Do you want to marry her?"

"If she isn't going to let me live with her anymore, I guess I'm going to have to marry her."

"Now there's an endorsement for romantic love. Jeez, Steve. If you love her, great, marry her. If you don't, this is as good a time as any to move on."

"Hell, Bree, how the hell am I supposed to know if I'm in love or not? I'm a guy, for God's sake."

"I'm going over to visit Meg. If you get it figured out, let me know."

He raised his hand in a half-hearted salute as I left. I was having a hard time feeling sorry for a guy who didn't know if he was in love with the woman he'd been living with for the last ten years. As far as I was concerned, Steve needed to get a grip.

I was standing in Meg's kitchen surveying the damage to her ceiling. There was a huge chunk of Homasote on the floor, dirt and mouse droppings were everywhere, and a bigger piece of ceiling was hanging, sifting more gross stuff onto the kitchen floor. Dusty cobwebs hung from the slats that used to support the original plaster ceiling.

"I didn't mean to do it." Meg wailed. "There's been a hole there forever, and I've always hated this ceiling, so I thought I'd just stick my finger in there and see what happened if I tugged on it. So I tugged, and this chunk of whatever this stuff is fell on my head. God! Who knew it would be so dirty up there? I'll never get this mess cleaned up. What am I going to do?"

"The first thing we should do is pull the rest of that panel down. Otherwise it's going to come down on someone's head. Crap is going to keep falling off it."

Meg nodded, reached up and grabbed an edge of the errant stuff, closed her eyes and pulled. It came away easily, bringing more droppings and spiders with it. Meg and I were coughing dust out of our lungs when Tom walked in.

Tom's a pretty understanding guy in most instances. He loves Meg's spontaneity and isn't usually bothered by the catastrophes that befall her. But he was also a cop with a stressful job, and he liked coming home to a tidy-ish house with at least the possibility of a meal. It would be a while before there was any food preparation in this kitchen again.

"Meg ..." he began.

"It was an accident," she broke in.

"Accident?" Tom looked incredulous. "You've been threatening to tear down this ceiling for the last five years."

"Well, I wasn't planning on starting today." Meg's voice raised an octave. "It just happened."

"Sweetheart, this didn't just happen, it was helped along. By you. I'll get these chunks of ceiling out of the way." He dragged the Homasote to the door.

"Where are you taking that?" I asked.

"The trash pile by the barn. Then I'm going to find my hidden stash of whiskey and have a drink. Like it or not, this is the beginning of a really big project that I've been hoping to put off indefinitely."

Tom went out to the barn, and I turned my attention to the mess. A film of grime covered the counter tops and chairs. A pile of paper scraps, mouse droppings and who knows what kind of hair littered the kitchen table. The floor was covered in more of the same.

"I think we should start high and work low," I said, "and maybe we should take everything movable out onto the porch and clean it before we bring it back in."

Meg went into the laundry room and came back with a couple of dust masks for us to wear. She grabbed kitchen gloves from under the sink and handed me the purple pair.

"These yellow ones are small," she said. "I think the purple ones will fit you better."

"Good. I like the purple ones better anyway."

We set to work carrying the chairs, toaster and what used to be clean dishes in the drainer out to the porch. The cookies that had been sitting on a plate on the kitchen table got trashed. I took the broom and swiped at the ceiling, trying to get the bits of dirt and cobwebs that were hanging from the slats.

We washed down the kitchen cabinets and then the tops of the counters using disinfectant spray. Meg used a whisk broom and dustpan to swipe the pile of crud off the table, and I cleaned the surface. Meg sighed when we got to the floor.

"I'm going to have to get another trash bag," she said. "There's a lot of crap in that ceiling."

We were just finishing up when Tom walked in with a stack of pizza boxes.

"My hero," Meg said.

"Mine too!" I grabbed the boxes from the top of the pile and set them on the table.

"I doubted you'd be in the mood for cooking after taking care of this mess, and I didn't want PB&J." Tom set the remaining boxes on the table next to my pile. "I'm going to call the kids."

Gemma, Pete, Louise and Jeremy thundered down the stairs to cries of "Pizza!"

Gemma took a moment to give me a hug, and then they all disappeared into the living room with a couple of pizzas and paper plates. The TV clicked on.

"You let them watch TV while they eat?' I asked.

"Only on pizza night." Meg said, standing at the table. "We still have to clean all the stuff out on the porch. I'd forgotten about that. I don't particularly want to start eating all my meals standing up."

"It can wait until after we've eaten." Tom reached into the fridge and brought out three beers. Then he hoisted himself up on the kitchen counter and sat with his plate in his lap.

I leaned on the edge of the counter, and Meg slid her butt onto the table.

"I hope the kids don't come in and see us doing this. It's hard enough to keep them off the counters."

We ate, tossed the boxes in the trash and cleaned the chairs out on the porch. I stretched as Meg and I finished wiping the last chair.

"I'm heading home," I said. "I've got some cleaning up of my own to do, but I'll be back tomorrow morning."

My phone was buzzing when I got in my truck. I searched through the discarded junk and clothing on the seat, finally finding it stuck in the passenger side door pocket. I pounced on the phone and flipped it open before it stopped ringing.

"Bree?"

"Yes?" I didn't recognize the voice.

"Sheriff Fogel. Beau's had an accident."

My heart either stopped beating or was beating so fast it was like a hummingbird in my chest. My voice was trapped in my throat.

"Bree? Are you there?"

"I'm here." My breath rushed out of me with the words. "Is he okay?"

"He'll be fine. He's had a concussion, and his leg is broken. They're keeping him in the hospital for now. He's refusing to call anyone himself, but he doesn't have any family to take care of him out here. You are the only contact I have."

"I'll tell his family. We'll get someone out there."

I was back in the house in an instant. Tom and Meg looked at me in surprise as I exploded into the room. Tom put down the pot he was drying, and Meg pulled off her yellow kitchen gloves.

"Beau's been hurt. He's in the hospital in California."

Meg sat down in a kitchen chair as Tom headed for the phone. He punched the speaker button, dialed the barracks and had the dispatcher find out which hospital Beau was in. It only took a couple of minutes before Tom was connected to the Sierra Nevada Memorial Hospital. The nurse was relaxed and friendly on the phone, and the mood in the kitchen lightened considerably. She transferred us to Beau's room.

"Yo, Bro. You're on the speaker phone with Meg and Bree, so keep it clean." Tom used his standard speaker phone warning. "I hear you've banged yourself up some. What happened?"

"That damned Fogel. I told him I didn't want my family worrying about me. I'm fine. I had an equipment failure is all. The staging collapsed."

"Your staging?" I tried to modulate my voice so I didn't let on that bells were going off in my head. Beau was compulsive about safety checking his equipment.

"Bree, don't make more of this than it is. Even I make mistakes once in a while."

"So what's the damage?" Tom asked.

"Broken leg, knock on the head. I'm not sure why they're keeping me so long. Something about making sure my head's okay. I'm fine, but they tell me I'm still too wonky to go home."

"Meg or I will come out and get you," Tom said. "No point in hanging around out there while you can't work."

A pang of guilt stung me. I hadn't told Tom or Meg that Beau was planning to stay in California. I had divided loyalties, and it stunk.

"I suppose so," Beau sounded reluctant.

"But I don't want Bree out here. It's not safe for her."

Tom rang off the phone and turned to me.

"I'm going," he said, "and don't fight me on this, Bree. You heard Beau, it's not safe for you out there."

"Tom?" Meg sounded unsure. "If you take time from work, we won't be able to take that trip we planned. I can go."

"What about the paper?" Tom looked perplexed. "You're only two days from your deadline."

"Bree can finish the paper." She didn't look happy.

"Stop it, you two. I'll go get Beau. For heaven's sake! What do you think is going to happen between the hospital and the airport? By the time anyone realizes I'm in town, we'll be back here."

"I don't like it." Tom looked at me and shook his head.

"Me either." Meg narrowed her eyes at me.

"Listen. It's not rational for either of you to leave now. I can write on the plane, in the hospital, wherever. I'll be in California, what, twenty-four hours at most? What could happen? Realistically, if anyone out there is looking for me, which I doubt, they aren't going to even know I've come and gone again."

"I hope you're right, Bree, or Beau is going to kill me," Tom said.

*I hope so, too.*

I glanced down the road as I pulled out of the rental lot at the Sacramento Airport. A black Ford pickup was just pulling away from the curb, but he motioned me to go ahead, so I pulled out in front of him and headed south down I-5, then east on I-80. The California sun was baking me, so I blasted the AC. The little Toyota I'd rented handled nicely, and I negotiated the traffic with surprising ease for a Vermonter. I hit the scan button looking for some traveling music. I wanted something upbeat to keep me awake and kill the boredom on the two-hour drive up the mountain.

The car was mounting the first of the foothills east of Rocklin when I glanced in the rear view and did a double take. I could swear the same black Ford that let me in back at the airport was two cars back. *Don't be stupid*, I told myself. *There's got to be a million black Fords in this city.* But the back of my neck started to crawl. I pulled into the slow lane and glanced back. *Shit.* The truck had changed lanes with me.

I pulled my cell phone out of my bag. Hell, I didn't know if using the phone was legal when you were driving in California. I shrugged. At least if I got pulled over I'd be safe from the truck behind me. With half an eye on the road, I searched back through my call history and found Sheriff Fogel.

"Trouble?" he asked before I even said a word.

"Got into town about an hour ago," I said. "There was a black Ford pickup waiting for me. I didn't realize it until a few minutes ago. Thought they were being nice when they waved me in front of them as I pulled out of the airport. What a putz I am."

"Normally I'd say head for someplace public, but I'm not sure that's the best thing to do in this case. If the guy who hired these thugs is as desperate as I think he is, they're just looking for a chance to take a pot shot at you. Frankly, I'm surprised they haven't tried to take you out on the freeway."

"Too much traffic. Someone might be able to ID them. That's my guess anyway. You want me to try and lose them?"

"How you going to do that?"

"Pull off onto Hwy 49 at the last second. If I go from the fast lane to the off-ramp without signaling they may not be able to react fast enough to catch me. Then I'll drive fast to the hospital where you can meet up with me and keep watch until I get Beau back into the car. What do you think?"

"I don't want you putting anyone in danger. If there's a chance that you'll cause an accident, forget it. I'll get a couple of local sheriffs to escort you, and we'll get you there and back that way."

I rang off and pulled back into the fast lane watching traffic as I drove past Roseville. Sure enough, the black truck followed. I slowed way down for a couple of miles, causing angry motorists to pass us on the right giving middle finger salutes. A mile from my exit I sped up, gradually increasing speed. The driver of the truck didn't appear to notice at first, dropping so far behind that I was afraid I was giving him too much room. But he noticed and increased his speed, too, gaining on me fast.

I checked traffic, saw my gap, and pulled the steering wheel hard to the right. The tires squealed, and somewhere a horn sounded. I took paint off the front fender grazing the yellow garbage cans filled with water that were grouped at the off ramp, but I made the exit. I glanced back and saw the black truck zoom past the off ramp, tires squealing and smoking as they tried to stop. I was just about to celebrate when the back-up lights lit up on the truck. *That idiot is going to back up on the freeway!*

I hit speaker and redial on the phone as I screamed up the off ramp.

"They're backing up down the freeway," I yelled at Fogel as I drove. "Do I get back on the freeway or head up forty-nine? You've got five seconds to decide."

"Get back on the freeway. There will be cruisers waiting for you just past the Foresthill exit."

I screamed through the red light, narrowly missing an oncoming Buick, *thank God*, and down the on-ramp across the intersection from the off ramp and back onto the freeway. *They know.* I needed to put as much distance as possible between us now. I had a feeling the kid gloves were off. I drove like a maniac, weaving in and out of traffic as fast as I was able. I kept checking the mirror, but it was a while before I saw them again. They were hanging back, keeping me in sight. *They're trying not to spook me again.* Which made me nervous, because that meant they had a plan for farther on down the road. Maybe for off the freeway.

I passed the Foresthill exit, and before I knew it, four cruisers surrounded me. The officer to my right motioned me to slow, and I brought it down to sixty-five. She gave me a thumbs-up. The road narrowed down to two lanes, and I was directed to drive in the left lane with the guy on the left dropping back. The black truck disappeared the minute the troopers showed up, and we made the drive up to Colfax and along Route 147 to Nevada City without incident.

Fogel met me outside the hospital, and I shook hands with and thanked my guardian angels. A tall black officer whose name tag read J. Russell said cheerfully, "Our pleasure, ma'am. More fun than I've had in a while."

Beau was propped up in bed watching a ball game when I walked in. A bandage was stuck to his head over his right ear, and a blue cast encased his leg from his foot to just above his knee. The cast was covered with graffiti, mostly girls' names as far as I could see. He turned as I stepped up to the bed and scowled at me.

"I told Tom not to let you come. Why won't you ever do as you're told?"

"Oh, you know me. I'm a tease. I figure by the time anyone knows I'm here we'll be gone again. I'm more worried about you getting dizzy and sliding off a roof. I know you, and given a day by yourself, you'll be figuring out how to work with a cast on. I'm taking you home as soon as they let you out of here."

I sat on the edge of his bed, careful not to bump his leg.

Beau smiled and shook his head. He reached over and took my hand.

"Damned if I'm not glad to see you, even if you shouldn't be here. Gonna kiss me and make it all better?"

I stopped holding my breath and kissed him.

Getting him out of the hospital wasn't as easy as I expected. The doctor talked vaguely of dizziness and memory loss. The nurse just shrugged her shoulders. Finally, Sheriff Fogel showed up, and the obstacles started to disappear. While Beau was signing papers and assuring the doctors he'd check in with his own medical team at home, Sheriff Fogel took me aside.

"Did Beau tell you the whole story about his accident? If you can call it an accident."

The worry was plain in Fogel's face, and my stomach clenched.

"What are you talking about?" I asked.

"The day before his accident he was visited by a couple of goons. They asked about you, and when Beau claimed ignorance, they threatened his life. The next day his second story staging collapsed. I asked the doctor not to release him until they were absolutely sure he wasn't going home alone. Luckily the administration here owes me a favor or two."

"Then it's not safe for Beau here either. We're on a flight out of here tonight. I've got to get to the house and clear out his stuff." I turned away, but Sheriff Fogel's hand on my shoulder stopped me.

"I took care of that the day he fell. Didn't need his house getting tossed again, so I had a deputy clear out the house, and we're watching it pretty closely. I'm worried these bastards will try and burn it down. I don't like the way they warn their victims."

"Was all the damage from the fall, or did they hurt Beau when they came to talk?"

"As far as I know they were civil enough on the first visit. Threats only."

"I'm getting us out of here, and he's not coming back until Lily's murder is solved, even if I have to break the other leg."

"Good girl." Fogel laughed.

Getting a man with a broken leg on the plane proved to be a challenge. I pushed the airport wheelchair down the jet way and parked it outside the door. Beau pushed himself up to stand on his good leg. He swayed a little, and I hurried to steady him. We managed to get through the door, but faced with the rows of first class seats we had to get past, I glanced at the flight attendant, nonplussed.

Beau took matters into his own hands. Sliding his arm from around my shoulder he used the backs of the seats like crutches and swung himself into economy seating where the attendant settled him into the first row of seats. I followed and plopped down in the middle seat next to him, hoping that the plane would be under-booked so no one would sit next to me.

Beau was laughing at me as I scowled at the passengers coming through the door from first class, trying to keep our spare seat open. He leaned over and put his mouth to my ear.

"It won't kill me if someone sits there you know. You could stop glaring at those poor people."

But I had stopped glaring anyway. A woman I recognized was standing at the head of the aisle scanning the plane. A plumpish redhead with Sara Palin glasses and a lost look on her face. The trouble was I couldn't remember where I knew her from. I scanned her face but couldn't figure out the connection. An elderly woman pushed past her and sat down in the seat next to me, and the redhead moved off down the aisle, leaving me with the uneasy impression that I had met her before.

I looked at Beau and noticed he was watching the other passengers as well. Tension was etched around his mouth. *He's watching for the people who threatened him.* I still hadn't told him that I knew his fall hadn't been accidental. He would just be angry with Fogel for telling me. Beau relaxed when the last piece of carry-on baggage bounced against the aisle seat, and the flight attendant locked the hatch shut.

"I take it you didn't recognize any of the passengers as your assailants."

Beau jerked his head up, a furrow forming between his brows.

"What are you talking about?" he asked.

"Fogel told me your accident probably wasn't."

"Damn him! Blasted busybody Sheriff. I was going to deal with those guys once and for all. Instead you show up, knowing far too much, and escort me home like I'm an invalid or a child." He sat with his arms crossed, the frown deepening.

"We were worried about you. Anyway, Tom's kids miss you, and there's stuff at your Vermont house that needs to be taken care of. And Beans. Don't forget Beans. He's having an identity crisis."

A smile crept on his face at the mention of Beans, and the muscles in his jaw relaxed.

"Yeah, okay. I can see how you'd think Beans would be missing me. I'll stay until I can walk again. How's that?"

"It's a deal."

Beau shifted uncomfortably in his seat. His cast and the limited space between our seats and the bulkhead weren't really compatible. I'd tried to shift so that he could angle his leg into my foot space, but the elderly woman who'd dropped into the seat beside me kept giving me dirty looks.

"Do you want to switch?" I asked him. "You could sit kind of sideways and rest your foot in the corner?"

"Would you kindly keep your voice down," the old woman snapped at me. "I'm trying to get my rest. I really don't understand people who expect everything to go their own way." She shut her eyes again, and I had to restrain myself. I wanted nothing more than to smack her, the old witch.

The flight attendant must have read my thoughts because she appeared in the aisle and leaned down to whisper in the woman's ear.

"There's an open row down a few seats," she said. "I can move you, and you'll be able to rest quietly by yourself."

I thought that was stretching it. There were people talking up and down the plane, and it wasn't exactly quiet.

"I don't want to sit at the back of the plane." Her eyes narrowed at the attendant. "Why don't you make these two sit back there? I'm sure he can move as well as I can." She pointed a bony old finger at Beau.

"Mr. Maverick is injured and needs to sit where he is."

"I don't want to move." The old biddy was sulking now.

"I heard you complain about the noise up here. It really would be quieter a few rows back."

I caught the attendant's glance, and she rolled her eyes to the ceiling.

"It's all right," I said. "We'll try to be more quiet."

"Should have made her move," Beau whispered. "We've got to put up with her for another four and a half hours." He closed his eyes and turned his face away from me.

"You could still change seats with me," I said.

"I'm not sitting next to that bitch."

His voice was quiet, but I was sure she could hear him. I didn't dare turn to look at her. She might take my head off. Sure enough, she snorted through her nose, but she didn't say anything. Didn't want to be caught eavesdropping, was my guess.

The mousy, red-haired woman I'd noticed earlier slid into the bathroom at the front of the plane. My mind automatically started flipping through the places I might have seen her in the past, but no bells went off. It bothered me that I couldn't place her.

I told myself not to be an idiot and closed my eyes, but the ball of unease sat in my stomach all the same.

The next morning Beau was settled in at home, and I was back at Meg's. Tom was pulling a double shift, and Meg figured we could have the entire ceiling down and the mess cleared up before he got home. Being Meg's best friend had perks; it wasn't every day I got invited to a demolition party. A bunch of tools were piled on the porch outside the back door.

"What's the sledge hammer for?" I asked as I walked in. She had cleared the kitchen of furniture. "Be kind of hard to whack the ceiling with that thing don't you think?"

"I just grabbed anything I thought we might need," she said. "Better too many tools than too few."

Pulling the Homasote down was the easy part. After getting mouse poop and other disgusting detritus dumped on my head a couple of times I learned not to pull the edge in front of me and we had the whole thing down in less than thirty minutes. The kitchen looked like a war zone with pieces of ceiling scattered among piles of dirt and unidentifiable bits and pieces, all of it disgusting.

Bits of cobweb and dirt hung from the slats that had been hidden by the board. Like many old homes, this one had once sported a plaster ceiling.

"You could re-plaster this and have an authentic ceiling," I said.

"I don't want an authentic ceiling. We're going to pull all this down, and I'm going to have exposed beams. I'll put sheet rock up between the beams to keep dirt from falling on the table while we eat."

"You're going to put up sheet rock?" My eyebrows threatened to skyrocket off my head. Not that I doubted Meg's ability to do anything she put her mind to, but she also owned the *Royalton Star*, a weekly newspaper that required most of her time to produce.

"I figured you could help with the sheet rock, and maybe you wouldn't mind pitching in and helping Deirdre with ads so we don't get behind. You've got like five articles all ready to go."

It was true. I had gotten ahead of myself. I didn't have any responsibilities in California and lots of time to mull things over in my head. The result had been a number of editorials that had the advantage of not being time sensitive. Meg was right. I did have time to help her.

"Okay," I said. "Let's get started pulling the slats down."

The slats were only marginally harder to get down than the Homasote. If I reached up, grabbed one and put a little weight on it, invariably the wood would come away into my hand. The only trouble was that the nails stayed behind. So Meg pulled down the slats, and I went along behind with the stepladder and a hammer and pulled the nails out. We were about an hour into that process when Meg's oldest, Jeremy, appeared in the doorway with a couple of his friends.

"Hey, Mom, we're kind of hungry."

"Sorry, Jer. The kitchen's out of order at the moment, but if you and your friends want to pitch in and haul this stuff out to dad's trash pile, it would speed up the process, and you could get something to eat."

I thought Meg was asking a bit much, but the boys must not have had anything more pressing to do, because they pitched in, piling slats onto the larger chunks of ceiling and dragging them out to the barn.

"I didn't think they'd do it," I said after the three had disappeared around the barn.

"Oh, they'll do anything for food," Meg said. "Anyway, they wouldn't be hanging around here if they had anything better to do."

After a makeshift lunch, Meg and I jumped into Tom's truck and headed to the local building supply company for sheet rock, screws and caulk.

"Um, Meg?" I ventured on our way home. "Do you know how to put this stuff up?"

"I saw them do it on *This Old House*, and I asked Scott about it when he was working on our barn. It's supposed to be really easy. You cut the wallboard, screw it up and then caulk around the edges. When you paint it the caulk blends in, and you can't tell it's not all one piece. Simple."

*Famous last words*, I thought to myself. I was having doubts about our ability to accomplish this within the required time frame, to say nothing of making it look okay. Yikes.

At 11:30 that night when Tom walked in, I was flat on my back six feet in the air on a plank of wood balanced between two folding ladders. I was holding a piece of sheet rock in place with my knees while I secured it in place with sheet rock screws. I placed the drill on the plank above my head and gingerly sat up. I didn't want to bash my head on a beam like the first time I tried sitting up.

"Uh, where's my wife?" he asked.

"She went uptown to buy some sandwiches. She fed the kids earlier, but we skipped dinner. She'll be back in a minute."

Tom stood looking at the ceiling. I couldn't read the look on his face. Either he was amazed, astounded or really pissed off and didn't want it to show. We'd gotten about half the sheet rock up. None of it was caulked yet, but on the whole I thought it was looking pretty good. The higher ceiling gave the room an airier look, and somehow it seemed brighter, at least to me.

"How'd you get wrangled into this job? Shouldn't you be getting sandwiches and Meg putting up the sheet rock?"

"It turns out Meg's not all that coordinated. She needed me to hold up the sheet rock while she screwed it in, but I can do it by myself. Why stop the whole production when we really only need one of us to get sandwiches?"

"Let me help you down from there. You've done enough for one day."

Tom jumped me down and I stretched my back until it cracked.

"I didn't realize how long I've been up there. I'm stiff."

"I guess Meg thought you could get this all done before I got home?" Tom shook his head. "I should know better than to tell her not to do something. "

Meg chose that moment to walk back in the house. She was juggling sandwiches and sodas with the dogs surging around her feet hoping for a windfall. Tom turned toward her, and she stopped. "Hi, honey," she said. "You're home early."

"It's almost midnight, Meg. I wouldn't exactly call that early. This is your revenge, is it?"

"What in the world would I need to get revenge for?"

"For me telling you not to pull down the ceiling."

"This isn't revenge. This is me doing what I feel needs to be done. I can make my own decisions about what I can and can't do." The smile Meg had on her face was open, playful. I wished I could be as self-confident as Meg was. She wasn't even nervous about defying Tom's wishes. If she thought something needed to be done, she had no doubts that she had every right to do it.

Tom laughed. "You're right about that! I hate having the kitchen torn up, but it looks like you'll have this done in a day or two." He surveyed the room. "There isn't any mess. How'd you manage that?"

"We cleaned as we worked," I said, "so the mess didn't get ahead of us."

We sat in the living room and ate sandwiches and chips. Yawns kept overwhelming me, and I was losing track of the conversation. I picked up the sandwich wrapper, paper plate and Coke can.

"I'm out of here," I said. "I can't keep my eyes open anymore. Are you going into work on the paper tomorrow, or is finishing the ceiling more important?"

"I'll come in for a while in the morning. What about you?"

"I'll be in. I can either work on the ceiling or the *Royalton Star*. You choose. I'll see you in the morning."

When I woke up the clock display said it was 3:00 a.m., and I was in pain. My neck hurt, and it was impossible to get into a comfortable position. I could barely turn my head at all. I sat up, groaning, "Jeez, this sucks," and added some choice swear words. I took my pillow and went downstairs to sit in my big armchair. I propped my pillow behind my neck, but it wasn't any better. The ibuprofen was on top of the refrigerator. Moving again wasn't high on my list, but as I couldn't get comfortable, I thought maybe it would take the edge off, so I dragged myself to the kitchen and swallowed three pills.

Back in the chair I was still having trouble getting comfortable. I stuffed the pillow behind my neck, tried shoving it behind my back. Nothing. *Damn*. I got up and slid a *Gilmore Girls* DVD into the player. At least that would distract me for a couple of hours. For two episodes I didn't miss a line. During the third I caught myself drifting once in a while. I think I slept through a good chunk of the fourth episode, still in pain but exhausted beyond caring.

At six in the morning I was moving around the house, whimpering from pain. I knew I couldn't drive myself to the hospital. I could barely move my head, for heaven's sake, but who could I call so early in the morning? It didn't seem fair to wake anyone, so I called the barracks to see what time Steve got off work and if he was free to take me.

Within twenty minutes Steve was at the door. I was dressed and had my medical card and cell phone in my pocket, but my shoes were untied. For the life of me I couldn't make myself try and bend down. Steve took one look at me and shook his head.

"You look like hell. Why didn't you call an ambulance hours ago?" He bent down and tied my shoes. "Get in the car. I'll feed your animals, and then we'll go."

I sat in the car trying not to cry. Every move I made hurt worse than the last. Forget moving, I hurt just sitting still. When Steve slid into the driver's seat I had my hands clenched in my lap trying to maintain. The first bump we hit caused my neck to feel as if it was on fire. I cupped the sides of my neck, trying to keep everything stable.

By the time I whooshed through the emergency room doors I would have given anything to be unconscious. I couldn't think straight, and it was hard to keep the tears out of my eyes. Steve's uniform got me through triage in record time. There are times when it's really handy to know a cop. Steve elected to stay in the waiting room when the nurse came to usher me into a glass fronted room. She pulled the curtain to give me some privacy and told me a doctor would be there shortly.

I sat in a chair usually reserved for family members. The thought of trying to lie on the gurney was too much. Lowering my head would use the muscles that were already screaming at me.

The doctor was young, but he was gentle with his hands and kind.

"What have you been doing?" he asked.

"Pulling down a ceiling and then putting a new one up."

"A lot of work above your head," He nodded. "That's typical. You've got a repetitive motion injury. Tort Collis, a muscle spasm in your neck. A little Valium, anti-inflammatory and time will take care of it. Oh, and get some physical therapy.

"Really?" I asked. "I have to do PT? That's a pain."

"If you want to get better and stay better, you'll do PT. What's the problem with that?"

"Appointments. Remembering them, taking time out of my day, driving to them, waiting around for them to be ready for me. It's a pain."

"Not as bad as that pain in your neck."

I swallowed the Valium with difficulty, for some reason swallowing set off the spasm in my neck. A male nurse came in and asked me to drop my pants.

"What?" I asked.

"The anti-inflammatory is an injection. It stings, and it will make your arm hurt for a couple of days. You've got more muscle in your butt, and it'll hurt less, but if you'd rather I'll put it in your arm."

I figured I was in enough pain and dropped my jeans.

"Whoa," he said. "That's plenty far enough, believe me."

So I took the shot in my rear, and Steve took me home.

Even after I'd taken the muscle relaxer and anti-inflammatory, I wasn't pain free. I was most comfortable sitting straight up, and I thought it would distract me to go down to the *Star* and work. The only problem with that was I couldn't turn my head. I might be able to work around that one, but I'd also taken Valium. Driving while impaired wasn't my style. I found a heating pad and hobbled upstairs like an old woman.

I was flat on my back staring at the ceiling. The Valium/Tylenol combo was wearing off, and the pain was coming back. I knew I should force myself into the bathroom to take some more; it just hurt so dang much to move. I also needed to pee. The pain I could ignore for a while, but the full bladder required immediate attention. I rolled onto my side, winced, and then I was off the bed and on my feet.

I shuffled into the bathroom, trying not to jar my neck or shoulder and did what I needed to do, which was to take the dang pills and empty my bladder. I contemplated the shower. The hot water would feel good on my neck, but the washing and toweling off part wouldn't be easy. I could feel the Valium kicking in, making me sleepy again, and decided against the shower.

I rolled back into bed trying for a comfortable position. It didn't matter if I stretched out or curled up, my neck would not give an inch. I ended up flat on my back again, staring at the ceiling and waiting for the pain to go away. My eyes started to feel heavy. *I bet that Valium isn't really a muscle relaxant,* I thought. *I bet they just use it to knock you out so that you don't feel the pain.* I had some fuzzy thoughts about doctors and injections before I was unconscious again.

Something heavy and warm was beside me on the bed. It kept bumping me, making my neck hurt. The cat pawed me on the arm, nicking me with her claw.

"Go away, Annabelle, that hurts."

"I'm not Annabelle." The voice was deep and unfamiliar.

I struggled to open my eyes but could not. I felt him lift me off the bed and wanted to call out, fight, anything. But all I did was slip back into oblivion, my mind filled with panic.

# Four

My neck hurt. I was sitting, reclined in a chair; the room was vibrating, and a low-pitched humming masked voices nearby. I kept my eyes closed knowing I was in trouble, trying to figure out just how bad it was. I couldn't move my head at all, not because of the pain, but because I was being restrained somehow. I couldn't figure it out. If I tried to feel things out with my hand, I'd tip them off to my consciousness.

"Sir, are you sure she's OK?" Concern was audible in the voice.

*Who are you?* I thought. *I do need help. Please help me.*

"She's fine. It's just the Dramamine. The stuff knocks her out cold. I told her not to take so much of it, but will she listen to me? No."

"Well, if you're sure."

I heard her move off. Shit. My brain was clearer now. I remembered thinking Annabelle had scratched me. *That was no cat scratch. Somebody's been drugging me.* The noises began to make sense to me. An airplane. I cracked my eyes and confirmed my suspicions. I was in the window seat of the first row, a bulkhead in front of me. Obviously, I'd been drugged.

I opened my eyes wide and looked at the thug that stood between me and my freedom. He was a tall, muscular man with a close-shaved head of light brown hair and hazel eyes. My first thought was that he hadn't shaved in at least a week, and then I realized he had carefully cultivated the look. His beard and mustache were too long to be sloppy living but too short to be considered a true beard. He wore a blue button-down shirt, open at the neck, and blue jeans. The smile he gave the flight attendant as she passed seemed calculated to disarm: charming and deadly.

I shifted in my chair and addressed him quietly.

"I have to pee. If you stick me with that needle again, I'll wet my pants. That will leave you to explain to everyone within smelling distance why the airplane stinks like urine." My hands explored the restraint around my neck as I talked. It was hard plastic with foam around the edges. No wonder I couldn't move my head. Now I knew why the emergency doc didn't give one to me, it didn't help the pain.

He looked at me and rubbed the furrow between his brows.

"You wouldn't."

"I would. You need to let me go pee."

"I wheeled you down the ramp in a wheel chair. They think you can't walk."

"I couldn't walk then because I was unconscious. Now that I'm conscious again, I can walk. I have to pee." I raised my voice, hoping the noise would make him nervous.

"Fine. Go pee, but I'm putting you out again as soon as you come back. I hate flying; I don't want to have to deal with you too."

I unbuckled and got unsteadily to my feet. A wave of nausea washed over me, and I put my hand to the bulkhead, breathing deeply.

"You okay?" he asked.

"Yeah," I said, closing my eyes and swallowing hard. "I just have to get my air legs."

"What the heck are air legs?"

"Air legs. You know, like sea legs but in the air."

"God." He shut his mouth and looked at me sourly as I stepped around his feet and legs.

We were only about three feet from the front toilet. I managed to shut the door before I started puking. Damn drugs. I ripped off the collar. It was impossible to puke properly with it on, and I was making a mess. I managed to empty my stomach and felt much better except for the huge mess I'd made. I cleaned up as best I could, peed just for good measure, and stood with my ear against the door.

I waited until I heard the flight attendants chatting and cracked open the door.

"Hey," I said quietly.

They turned toward me, and the blond looked from my face to the collar in my hand and back.

"Are you supposed to take that off?" She asked.

"I need your help."

She turned as if to get the guy I was with.

"No!" I cried.

She startled and turned back to me, her face grave.

"You can't tell him," I said. "Do you have a pen and paper?"

The second flight attendant, a petite brunette who looked to be in her mid-twenties, handed me a pencil and the pad she wrote her drink orders on. Both the women looked worried, and the brunette kept looking furtively at the door to the cockpit. I wrote Fogel's name and number on the paper along with my own.

"Can you contact this man? He's a sheriff in California. Tell him I'm on this plane and where and when we're landing. OK?"

The blond looked at me with pity in her eyes.

"You do know that causing panic on an airplane is a federal offense, don't you? This isn't a game."

"Listen," I said. "I don't know what that guy I'm with told you, but I was abducted from my home. I need you to call Sheriff Fogel. If it's a hoax, you can have me arrested at the airport."

"Lucky for you," the brunette said, "we have to take this seriously, but boy, will you be in trouble when we land."

The blond looked disgusted. I could tell if it were up to her they'd be tearing the paper into little shreds and putting me back in my seat.

"I can't go into the cockpit with you in the bathroom. You'll have to go back to your seat." The brunette was trying to push me back into the main cabin.

"Wait. Help me get this thing back on."

The blond strapped me into the neck brace so tightly I thought my head would pop off. I slid past the thug and dropped into my seat. He didn't give me two seconds before he whipped an injection pen out of his pocket and got me in the arm with it. As I blanked out I heard the blond's voice. "Can I talk to your friend for a moment, sir?" And then I was gone.

The next time I woke up I was upside down, my stomach over the thug's shoulder in bright sunlight. I immediately threw up all over his backside.

"Shit. You could have warned me," he said, but he kept running, puke flying off the back of his pants.

"I'm going to puke again if you don't put me down." I wasn't really, but I thought it was worth a try.

He grunted but kept running. The combination of the drugs, the motion, and lack of food was making me woozy. I really just wanted to lie down somewhere until the world stopped spinning. I tried to look around at the upside down view, but nothing was making much sense and looking just made my head spin worse. I felt more than saw the light change as we ran into the open door of what must have been a hangar.

We slowed, I heard the click of a car door, and he dumped me on a leather-covered rear seat and slammed the door. He was outside the car, swearing about the vomit.

"Get in, Richard. We don't have time for this." An unfamiliar male voice occupied the driver's seat. We can get the car cleaned later."

The front door slammed shut, and Richard turned to me.

"Sit still, and don't do anything stupid. I'm not interested in going to jail over this."

"If you're not interested in going to jail, then you probably shouldn't have forcibly abducted me from my home, to say nothing of the damage you're inflicting on my neck. I'm supposed to be at PT." I knew I sounded like a whiner, but I couldn't help it.

I didn't have a clue how long I'd been out of commission. Richard could have put me out any number of times before I'd gained consciousness. I didn't have a clue where the heck I was, although I assumed it was probably California. After all, that was where Lily Wallace had died.

"Where are we?" I asked.

"You'll find out soon enough."

"OK. How about who are you?"

"I'm Richard Hambecker, this is Moose."

That surprised me. He must be pretty confident about what he was doing if he was willing to give me his name.

The car pulled slowly out of the hangar and made its way toward a military-style gate surrounded by chain link fence with razor wire running along its top. As we approached, Hambecker turned to me, an EpiPen in his hand.

"I really don't want to stick you with this thing again, so give me your word you'll be quiet, and I won't."

*Hell no, I'm not going to stay quiet.*

"You'd better stick me, because I'm sure as hell not going to stay quiet." *Shit. I should have lied to him.*

"Nah," said the driver named Moose. "You don't have to do that. I'll just raise the privacy window. He hit a button and a tinted window rose in front of me.

"Shit! Shit! Shit!" I said aloud.

"Now, now. No need to be rude." The voice came through a speaker. "There's no point in yelling, because all I have to do is hit a switch, and the guy at the gate won't be able to hear you.

We pulled up to the guardhouse where a uniformed young man looked at a clipboard and made as if to wave us through. Then his hand went to his belt, and my hopes climbed into my throat. He talked for a minute on his two-way radio and walked to the window.

I slid over next to the door, ready to roll. I didn't think either of the guys in the front seat could see me through the privacy window. If this was like most cars, then it was the passenger's privacy the window was in place to protect, not the driver's. I slid my fingers under the handle and pulled. Nothing. I pulled harder. Still nothing. I pulled and pushed on the door at the same time.

"Shit!"

I stared at the guard standing at the driver's window. He looked overheated in his uniform. Heat waves were radiating off the tarmac making the chain link fence shimmer.

"This Senator Wallace's car?" The guard's voice was tinny and far away through the speaker.

"Yes." The driver's voice.

"There's something going on at the main terminal, but I was told that the senator was cleared. So you can go."

The gate slid back and we rolled forward onto a deserted surface street.

"Sorry about that," Hambecker's voice came through the speaker this time. "The rear doors have child locks on them. We don't use them for the senator, of course, but they do come in useful on occasion."

I stuck my tongue out at him through the tinted window and looked out on the world. All the windows were tinted, fading color and reducing the contrasts of the world outside. A thrill of recognition ran through me. I knew where we were. Of course, it helped that it hadn't been that long since I came to get Beau. I was in Sacramento.

I wondered if Sheriff Fogel had been at the airport when we landed. How had we gotten out of the plane?

"Hey!" I yelled at the guys in the front. "I want to talk to you."

The privacy window slowly descended, and Hambecker turned to me.

"Yep?" He said.

"Hammie, how'd we get out of the airplane? Wasn't there someone there to meet us?"

"What did you call me?" A flush was showing above his collar.

"Uh, Hammie?" There was a red flush crawling up my neck now, too.

"Don't do it again. What did you ask me?"

"What happened back there?"

"You've got a wire in your neck brace. I heard you talking to the flight attendants."

Figures. He had me wired. What a schmuck I was.

"I still don't understand how we got out of the plane."

"They asked me to let everyone else off the plane before we got you out. So I let about half of them go. Then I hoisted you out of your seat, created a huge traffic jam, and forced my way toward the back of the plane. Caused a huge commotion. Popped an emergency door, and we slid to the tarmac where I stole a luggage tram which I drove as far as I thought was safe and then hoofed it the rest of the way to the VIP hangar. Not how I expected I'd be using my many skills." There was a tinge of regret in his voice.

"You make it sound like you didn't enjoy that."

"I don't usually find myself on the wrong side of the law. It goes against my nature."

"Then why do it?"

"Good question." But he didn't tell me, and I couldn't get him to say anything else.

Thirty minutes later we drove into an underground lot in downtown Sacramento. The men hustled me between them into an elevator. When the doors slid open we were on the uppermost floor of a hotel. At least I assumed it was the top floor, since the elevator didn't go any higher. Hammie and The Driver, which was how I thought of them, quick-stepped me down the hall to the last room.

The view wasn't spectacular like it was from the hotel in Washington, but the room itself was very tasteful, and I'd venture to guess very expensive. There was a plush bed with a faintly shimmery duvet cover and at least eight pillows, a tasteful couch in the same peach tones across from a TV the size of a picture window.

Hammie was not happy. He had his back to the room, looking out the window as he talked on his cell. His replies were terse. I was sitting cross-legged on the comfy bed, leaning against the head board with a *People* magazine while Hammie talked and The Driver sat in a chair by the door, snickering.

"He should know better," The Driver said.

"Know better than what?" Now that we were here, and the drugs were wearing off I was feeling strangely calm. I wondered if I was in shock, but the strangest thing was the pain in my neck was totally gone.

"To think he's got any control over the situation. He thinks if he just sticks this out, he'll get his life back. He's just getting deeper and deeper in."

I looked from The Driver to Hammie and back again.

"What's your name? I think Hammie told me, but I don't remember. I can't keep thinking of you as The Driver. It doesn't seem right."

"Marshall, but my friends call me Moose. I'm the brains." He laughed at his own joke.

"Just what is Hammie getting deeper into? Something to do with me, I'd guess."

"I'm not allowed to tell you." Moose looked regretful. "But I imagine you'll know before too long."

"It's too bad you can't slam a cell phone," I said to Hammie as he clicked his phone shut. "That would probably make you feel much better."

"Hah! Nothing could make me feel better at this point. What size are you? I've got to go buy you a dress."

"What do I need a dress for?"

"We're going to a jazz concert."

"A jazz concert? That's interesting." In the back of my brain I was thinking this could only be a dream.

"So, what size?"

I told him my size, and he took off, leaving Moose in charge of me. I picked up the phone next to the bed and dialed the front desk. Before anyone could answer Moose had taken the phone from me and replaced it in the receiver.

"What the hell do you think you're doing?"

"I'm going to need to shave my legs if I'm wearing a dress. I was going to ask the front desk to send me a razor."

"Hang on." Moose opened a door I hadn't noticed and walked into an adjoining room. He came back with a disposable razor.

"Here. It's new. I usually travel with several."

I hid my amazement and got to my feet. I swayed for a moment, still kind of woozy from the drugs. I made it into the bathroom and locked the door. Then I put the toilet lid down and sat with my head between my knees, hoping I wouldn't pass out while locked in the bathroom.

I managed my shower by leaning against the wall whenever dizziness overtook me. I shaved my legs, but I had the feeling that I wasn't doing a very good job. Hell, who was going to be looking at my legs anyway? Certainly not Hammie, not that I'd want Hammie to look at them. He wasn't my type. All brawn, a get-things-done-and-damn-the-consequences kind of guy.

I was back on the bed, wearing a hotel robe and a towel in my hair, when Hammie returned. He tossed a pretty blue dress with a matching jacket on the bed along with a Macy's bag. I grabbed the bag and pulled out a bra, panties and a pair of nylons.

"I'm impressed. How'd you know what size bra I wear?"

"I'm a good judge of a woman's figure. Lots of experience."

Moose snorted.

"He called me on the phone while you were in the shower, so I picked the lock and checked the tags in your clothes. You know that bra you were wearing is so old I could barely make out the size? That couldn't be giving you enough support."

"I do not want to discuss my undergarments with strange men." I looked at Hammie. "How long before we have to leave? I'm going to need some makeup."

"I draw the line at buying cosmetics. You can go without."

"I'll buy her makeup," Moose said. "I've got a basketful of sisters. I've bought all kinds of female stuff."

I made Moose a list of what I needed, and he went off with a grin on his face. I could swear he was enjoying himself, and I couldn't drum up an ounce of fear. The situation was too unreal. If anyone had wanted me dead, there had been plenty of time to accomplish that when I'd been unconscious. It seemed like whatever the original plan had been, it had blown up in Hammie's face, and he didn't know how to deal with buying dresses and taking hostages to jazz concerts.

I took the dress and the undergarments into the bathroom and changed out of the robe. I left the pantyhose unopened. I didn't plan on wearing hose to my own parents' funeral; no way was I wearing them for these goons. I pulled the soft material of the dress over my head and marveled at how well it fit me. Hammie really did know his clothes, much better than I did, as a matter of fact. The dress was a three-quarter sleeve with a high-waisted, formfitting, V-neck bodice that fell into a full skirt of soft folds that swayed around my calves. *Nice*, I thought, swooshing the skirt back and forth.

Then I looked at my feet. The only shoes I had were the sneakers I'd been wearing on the plane. How did I get those sneakers on, when I'd been lying on my bed in just my socks? *Hammie put them on you. Probably before he carried you out of the house.* I felt vaguely disturbed. Was I in denial or something? Why was I merrily putting on a dress to go to a concert when just this morning I'd been abducted from my home? *There's something wrong with me.* But I put that thought aside and sashayed out into the main room to find out what Hammie intended to do about shoes.

I was fuming. The makeup and shoe issues had been solved, and Hammie had gone to his room and come back looking very respectable in a grey suit. Then he had gotten Moose to take a clear zip tie and an O-ring to handcuff us together. He wrapped the zip tie around my wrist, crossed both ends through the O-ring around Hammie's wrist and then threaded the free end through the lock. Standing, our jacket sleeves hid the cuff fairly well, but I had the feeling that resting our arms on the theatre seat would expose our wrists to the world.

"Hammie, I can't go to a concert handcuffed to you," I said. "Someone will notice."

"Will you stop calling me Hammie," he said for the tenth time. "My name is Richard. The only person who will notice will be my fiancée, and with my luck she'll notice that we're holding hands, not that we're cuffed together, and that will be the end of that." He looked down at my wrist ruefully. "This hasn't been the most stellar day."

He led me out of the hotel room, dragging me along by my wrist. I felt like a rag doll, bouncing along behind him with Moose following behind laughing to himself.

"Slow down, would you Hammie? I can't walk that fast in these shoes."

He stopped at the elevator and looked at the shoes. They were sexy as hell and matched the blue of the dress perfectly. A crease appeared between his eyebrows. He probably thought all women wore four-inch heels. The elevator dinged, and the doors opened.

Hammie and I sat in the back of the car on the way to the concert, not that we had any choice. There wasn't room for two in the seat next to the driver. Anyway, it was a limo, and people would expect parties arriving in limos to emerge from the back of the car. I tried not to think about Hammie's thigh, which was touching me, or the feel of his hand next to mine, not that I was at all tempted to cheat on Beau. Hammie was the kind of guy women follow with their eyes, and it was distracting to be sitting next to him. His personality radiated out and enveloped any woman who happened to be near, and at the moment that woman was me.

Thanks to our long-sleeve jackets, we managed to get ourselves seated in the theatre without anyone commenting on the fact that we were linked together. There wasn't anyone else seated in our row. We were well toward the front of the auditorium, but not so far forward we'd have to strain our necks to see the performers. The rows around us were beginning to fill. Hammie fidgeted and glanced at his watch with a faint frown.

"Who are you expecting?" I asked.

"My boss and his entourage. My fiancée is supposed to be here, too, but I'm hoping the senator discouraged her from coming."

"What? You don't want your fiancée to see you handcuffed to another woman? Where's your sense of adventure, Hammie?"

"Will you please stop calling me Hammie? My name is Richard."

"Richard? I think Hammie suits you better."

Hammie gave me an exasperated look. He looked past me down the aisle, and his face cleared. Then he scowled.

"I take it she's here?"

"The blonde in the red coat."

The blonde shot me a look of pure hatred before she took her seat.

"Wow," I said to Hammie. "I'd watch out for her later, if I were you. She's out for blood." Hammie rolled his eyes and leaned across me to shake hands with the balding bespectacled man who had seated himself beside me.

"Senator," he said.

"Richard, a pleasure as always." He shifted his gaze to me. "And this must be our guest, Ms. MacGowan. Pleased to finally make your acquaintance. I hope Mr. Hambecker and Mr. Moore have been treating you well. I have something I'd like you to do for me." He nodded his head and squeezed my left hand that was on the armrest beside him.

"Gosh, Senator … I'm sorry, but I don't know your name. Are you in the habit of abducting your guests and keeping them handcuffed?" Funny, I wasn't angry with Hammie, but this guy got my blood boiling.

"Hush now. My name is Senator R. Carl Wallace." He glanced around and went on in an undertone. "I can't afford to lose you again. I need to talk to you, and I don't have time to spend chasing you across the country. I apologize, but I think you'll soon see that I have the best of intentions."

I raised my eyebrows, working at composing a suitable comeback, but the lights dimmed and the two guitarists came to the stage. They played some perfectly beautiful jazz; but the theatre was warm, and the drugs still must have been affecting me because I felt myself sliding toward unconsciousness again. Hammie leaned into me, keeping me upright with his shoulder, and I struggled to keep my eyes open and failed.

I might have fallen into a dead sleep and stayed that way for the entire concert except that the auditorium exploded into applause as the vocalist arrived on stage. She was a majestic black woman with a fabulous voice that vibrated in my chest. My eyes came open and stayed open as she sang. I'd never heard anything like her before.

After the encore, Hammie led me into the lobby. There were a couple of men from Senator Wallace's entourage close behind me, and the blonde in the red coat was behind them trying to push by. A State Trooper in dress uniform made his way toward us, and Moose appeared beside me, reached his arm around and clipped the nylon handcuff which fell to the floor as Moose whisked me away from Hammie and the Trooper and escorted me out of the lobby and into the waiting car.

"Why did you bother handcuffing me at all if you were going to take it off at the first sign of trouble? I sat through that whole concert handcuffed to Hammie, even though there was no way for me to get away unless I climbed over the backs of chairs in these damn shoes, and then you uncuff me right in the lobby where I could easily get away? I don't understand you people."

Mostly I was disgusted with myself. Why hadn't I screamed or made a fuss? The perfect moment to get rescued, and I'd done nothing. Stupid.

Marshall Moore, aka Moose, locked me into the back of the limo and slid into the driver's seat. He rolled down the privacy window. I wanted to hate Moose and Hammie. It felt stupid not to hate them, but I couldn't get the emotion to build. They were nice to me, and I had the distinct feeling that they weren't happy about being involved in whatever this was.

I knew it had to be about the death of the woman. I knew they probably were privy to the details. I hoped they hadn't done it. It was obvious that Hammie could have done it. He seemed to have some very specialized skills. Trained in special services? I thought it was likely. I didn't want them to know who killed Lily Carver Wallace, but I couldn't get around the fact that they probably did.

"You look like you smelled something rotten," Moose said to me. "What's up?"

"What's up? Don't pretend innocence with me, Moose. I'm in California listening to a jazz concert with a Senator Wallace, who I've never even heard of before, instead of at home in Vermont taking care of my farm."

"When you put it like that." Moose shrugged. "It does sound a little fishy. Powerful men like the Senator are used to getting what they want and don't worry too much how they make it happen. He pulled a lot of strings to get Hambecker on his payroll just so he can make things happen."

"So Hammie has a price. That's not surprising; everyone has a price." But I was surprised and disappointed. Somehow I thought he wouldn't be motivated by money. *Naive*, I told myself. *Swayed by a pretty face.*

"Wallace isn't paying Richard," Moose turned toward me. "He's got something on Richard's dad. I don't know the details, but I think he paid someone to blackmail him, and Richard ended up on Wallace's payroll as part of the deal."

"Hammie's dad is being blackmailed? Who is he?"

"Do you remember the State Trooper who was approaching you when I removed you from the lobby?"

"Removed me from the lobby. That's an interesting way of putting it. He was a handsome, older man. Had a dress uniform on."

"That's Richard's dad."

"That's Richard's dad," I repeated. The implications weren't lost on me. I could see the red-coated blonde and his father, both descending on Hammie, expecting explanations about the strange woman he'd been with.

"That dress looks exceptionally good on you," Moose said. "Richard did a nice job picking that out. I wonder what Paris would say if she knew he picked it out for you."

"Paris? The blonde red coat?"

Moose laughed.

"That's good," he said, "but she probably thinks he's the red coat, sitting with another woman at the concert."

"If she knows the Senator, then she knows he had no choice."

"That won't stop her from holding it against him. Paris is used to getting what Paris wants." Moose glanced out of the window, got his body in motion and was out of the car in an instant.

I glanced out to see Wallace, flanked on one side by Hammie and the other by the red coat. Paris's face was stony, Hammie looked like he wanted to be anywhere else, but Senator Wallace was smiling and talking animatedly. Hammie slid in beside me as the Senator skillfully guided Paris to another car.

# Five

Hammie normally sat in the front with Moose unless we were handcuffed. His presence beside me left me wondering if Wallace had requested it or if Hambecker felt the senator would have expected it. Hammie sat back and closed his eyes. He looked relaxed, but a twitch at the outer corner of his eye made me think the stress was getting to him.

"Your girlfriend doesn't look happy," I said, and Moose snorted in the front seat.

Hammie opened his eyes and scowled at Moose.

"It's going to take some time to convince her that this wasn't my idea," he said. "Meanwhile, my ass is grass." He shrugged. "I've lived through worse."

"Too bad she's not more understanding." I wondered if he would notice that I was pumping for information.

"Paris? She's all right. She doesn't want some other woman holding hands with her guy. I kind of appreciate that in a woman. It would make me nervous if she was okay with it."

We drove back into the parking lot under the hotel, and the men escorted me up to my room. Moose tossed me an oversized T-shirt with "Sacramento" emblazoned across the front, and I went into the bathroom to change out of the swishy dress and feet-numbing shoes. Moose had picked up a toothbrush and toothpaste earlier, and I took care of the usual nighttime routine before I walked back into the room. The T-shirt covered all the essentials with a couple of inches to spare, but I was self-conscious anyway, so I slipped under the covers and sat propped against the headboard with the TV remote.

Hammie turned from the window where he'd been looking out on Sacramento.

"Not much to see, is there? Sacramento is a pretty small town," I said.

"I wouldn't say Sacramento is small." He looked down at the street below. "Used to be a much smaller town."

"Compared to say, Boston or Chicago, it's still pretty small."

"At least they don't roll up the sidewalk at seven any more." He looked at the remote in my hand. "I suggest you keep your viewing down to a minimum. We have an early wake-up tomorrow." He looked at Moose and tilted his head toward me before he stepped through the adjoining door.

Moose got up and walked over to me. He fished around in the pocket of his jacket and pulled out a couple of zip ties.

"Sorry about this," he said. "We can't risk you taking a walk in the night." He pulled back the covers and slid the zip ties around my ankles, linking them together. Then he left through the adjoining door, leaving it cracked open.

"Hey!" I shouted. "What if I need to pee in the night? What if there's a fire?"

"That's why I left the door open, so I could hear if you call out. Don't worry, if there's a fire the sprinkler system will kick on. You're more likely to drown than burn. Goodnight."

"Goodnight?" I grumbled under my breath. "How the hell am I supposed to have a good night?"

I did eventually go to sleep, but every time I tried to roll over I woke up. Around two a.m. I got totally fed up and started yelling for Moose. He came in sleepily rubbing his eyes and cut the zip tie off my ankles. When I came back from the bathroom, he was asleep on my bed, and I stood there nonplussed. How was I going to sleep with a huge guy sleeping sprawled across my bed? I was looking at the bed, thinking about which side would give me more room, when my brain finally woke up, and I looked at the door. I was free.

I slid back into the bathroom and pulled on my jeans, socks and bra. I kept the big shirt, since it smelled a hell of a lot better than the one I'd worn on the plane. I crept back into the room, watching to make sure Moose didn't move, and picked up my shoes. I wondered where the keys to the car were but didn't bother to look for them. I doubted I could get that limo out of the parking lot.

The click the lock made when I turned the deadbolt sounded way too loud, and I stood frozen for a moment listening for movement from either of the men. I could see Hammie through the open door to the next room. He was stretched out on the bed, dressed in his jeans and a white T-shirt. He looked big and rumpled and vulnerable, so sexy he knocked me for a loop. I shook my head and slipped into the hall. I avoided the elevator and went through the fire door to the stairs.

I sat on the top step and pulled on my sneakers, lacing them tight and double-knotting the bows. Then I started down the stairs quietly. I didn't want to draw attention to myself. When I finally shot through the door at the bottom flight of stairs I realized I'd made a mistake. I was in the parking garage. I'd been shooting for the main entrance.

I weighed the risk of taking the elevator back up to the lobby against how much faster it might be than climbing back up the stairs. Speed won, and I punched the elevator button and waited. It didn't come. I paced for a couple of minutes hoping it would show up before I walked back over to the stairwell. I grabbed the handle and tugged, but it didn't budge. Shit. A sign next to the door caught my attention. No access to the shopping mall or hotel between midnight and six am. Great. I was beginning to think I should have stolen the keys to the limo after all. I trotted down the rows of cars, following the exit signs. Panic was starting to rise in my chest, and I worked at pushing it aside.

"Be like Hammie," I said aloud. "Cool and calm. Work with the circumstances." I jogged up the exit ramp, trying to tread softly so I could hear if anyone was behind me. Out on the street rain was falling softly so that the street and traffic lights reflected off the roadway. I stopped and looked around me. I was on the back side of a mall; a Macy's towered above me. I could see the hotel rising above a bank of stores, but I was on the wrong side of the block to access it.

I jogged to the corner. The cross street ran under the mall, coming up on the other side, so I turned and jogged down the incline. My neck was starting to hurt again, and every step sent a sharp pain through my neck and down my shoulder. At the bottom of the dip I slowed to a walk, conserving my energy to get up the hill.

The street crossed over the mall at the top of the rise, and I realized I'd made another mistake. The entrance to the hotel wasn't on this side either. Maybe there wasn't a way to get into the hotel from the street? But that didn't make sense either. Surely hotel guests wanted to go shopping, too. They'd need a way to get back into the hotel, right?

I jogged along the mall, running out of time, knowing that the hotel was the only place I'd be able to get into this early in the morning. I just needed a phone, one lousy phone, but effing cell phones had made pay phones obsolete.

I turned the corner again. I'd been three quarters of the way around this block; this had to be where the entrance was. Sure enough, the doors into the shopping mall also led to the hotel lobby. Jackpot. I walked toward the doors and was rewarded with a quiet swoosh as they slid open automatically. *Keep your cool, Bree, this is the dangerous part.*

I skirted around the glass atrium in the entrance of the shopping mall and scanned the lobby of the hotel. Vacant. I couldn't even see anyone at the desk. I was about to make a break for the phone sitting on a counter near the front desk when the elevator dinged. I slid back, hiding behind a potted palm. Hammie and Moose walked out of the elevator.

Hammie was scanning the lobby much the way I had been a moment before. Moose was following along behind him with a hangdog look on his face. Obviously, Hammie had read Moose the riot act when I'd gone missing. Hammie turned and spoke to Moose. Moose broke away and headed toward the street. I crouched behind the pot, heart racing. Either he would see me, or Hammie would. *Damn.*

"Damn, Damn, Damn." It was a moment before I realized I'd said it out loud. Well, Shit. Now the cat was out of the bag. Moose had turned toward me, but Hammie was looking the other way. I followed his gaze and realized he could see me in the reflection in the polished gold of the elevator doors.

We locked eyes in the reflection. Hammie narrowed his eyes. He mouthed something I couldn't hear and began to turn. Something in me cracked, and I launched myself at Hammie. I skated across the polished tile floor, jumped onto his back, anchoring my right arm around his neck and clinging like a monkey. He staggered forward, grabbed at the arm I had cutting off his air supply, lost his balance and fell over backward on top of me.

We lay there for a minute. I assumed Hammie was getting his bearings. The only reason I wasn't up and running was that I was stuck underneath him. I tried wriggling away, but my leg was trapped between his arm and his side, and he wasn't giving me an inch.

Hammie wrapped a hand around my wrist, rolled over, and pushed himself upright without letting me go. Moose plucked me off the ground, and I looked up to see a horrified desk clerk reach for the phone.

# Six

Hammie walked over and spoke to the desk clerk. The phone was replaced in its cradle, quiet words were exchanged, and I saw money change hands.

I was sobbing and shaking uncontrollably. Moose had his arms wrapped around my waist, and he sat down on one of the plush couches, probably to keep from dropping me. I collapsed on top of him, all the energy draining out of me. I was face down in the couch cushion, my midsection across his knees, choking and crying like a child.

"Jeez, girl. You're going to flood the place."

"I hope you drown," I said into the cushion.

"Hey. That's not a nice thing to say to a guy who bought you make up. I'm just doing my job."

"Well, your job sucks. I hate both of you."

"Come on," Hammie said from above me. "Let's go get some sleep."

"Have you ever tried to sleep with your legs tied together? It's impossible." I'd stopped crying. I wasn't full of rage anymore, but anger burned in my chest. I wanted my life back. I wanted revenge.

Hammie picked me up off of Moose and set my feet on the floor. They lock-stepped me over to the elevator, and I could feel the desk clerk's eyes on my back.

"What did you tell him about me?" I asked Hammie.

"That you were my sister, our mother had died, and you were out of your mind with grief."

"Well, at least you didn't tell him I was crazy."

Moose and Hammie exchanged glances.

"Oh, so you did tell him I'm crazy. Great. I'm never coming to this hotel again."

Back in the room I noticed my neck was hurting again. The effects of whatever drug Hammie had been pumping into me were wearing off. That was going to make it even more difficult to get comfortable.

"I don't want my legs tied up again. I can't sleep like that."

"How do you expect us to keep you in the room?" Hammie asked.

"Not my problem. You want to keep me in here, then sit in a chair by the door. Be a proper bodyguard."

"Moose and I need our sleep. We've had a rough couple of weeks."

"I bet." I imagined one of them must have pushed Lily off the bridge and that his conscience had been keeping him awake.

"Okay, Moose can cuff our wrists together. We can sleep like that."

I opened my mouth to protest, but Hammie cut me off.

"It's either your legs or our arms. Choose your poison. I'm done talking about it."

I picked wrists, not because I was looking forward to sleeping with Hammie, but because at least I'd be able to move around some. Moose pulled another zip tie and an O ring out of his bag.

"Which arm?" he asked.

"I sleep on my side," I said.

"You?" Moose raised his eyebrows at Hammie.

"Stomach."

"Right arms together then."

Moose cuffed our right arms, and it was damned awkward with my arm pulled across my body. I turned and faced the opposite direction, which at least freed me up. I slid off my shoes without untying them. I pulled up my shirt and fumbled with the button to my jeans with my left hand. No way I was going to try using my right hand and have Hammie's fingers that close to my zipper.

"Hey! Hold on," Hammie sounded panicked. "Got to keep the clothes on."

"I am not sleeping in my jeans. Anyway, this shirt covers everything."

"I don't like it."

"What? You think I'm going to jump your bones in your sleep? Give me a break."

I got the zipper undone and kicked off my jeans while Hammie looked the other way. I sat on the edge of the bed and slid my feet under the covers. Hammie stood next to me.

"You have to move over," he said.

"I'm not moving over, this is my side of the bed."

"Fine."

He put his knee on the edge of the bed and straddled me.

"Get off." I didn't know if I was outraged or turned on.

"Don't worry, I'm not molesting you." The sarcasm in his voice stung.

He pushed himself over me and landed on the bed on his back, which pulled my arm across my body. Then he rolled over onto his stomach, which pulled me over, my arm across his body. My head on his shoulder.

*My God, he's solid muscle.*

"Hey!" I said. "Give me my hand back."

I tried to pull my arm back, but he didn't budge.

"Nope. This is how I sleep, and you don't feel half bad on top of me."

"Moose, help me."

Moose shook his head at us and cut the zip tie.

"Get comfortable," he said.

"I can't. I sleep on my side. I won't be able to sleep facing Hammie, and I can't sleep facing away from him with my arm pulled backward."

"Front or back, then, you choose. And hurry up, I'm tired, not much night left."

I chose to sleep on my back, and Moose cuffed our left wrists together.

"I'll never be able to sleep like this," I muttered.

I woke with sunlight on my face. I was on my side with Hammie's arm around me. He was holding me close, his breath deep and even against my hair. Shit.

"Hammie! Wake up!"

I tried to push his arm off me, but he held me close.

"Hammie!"

"Go back to sleep," he murmured. "I'm not ready to get up."

"I'm not Paris. You need to wake up."

"I know you're not Paris. Go to sleep."

"What are you doing clutching me if you know I'm not Paris?"

"Paris is not nearly this nice to sleep with. I'm not molesting you or anything. Can't you just let me sleep? Fifteen more minutes." His breathing got regular again.

*Why can't I just fall asleep like that?*

I lay with Hammie's arm around me thinking about Beau. Beau's body temperature ran high. He got overheated if we slept too close together. We snuggled, but when Beau went to sleep he was normally covers off, sprawled over his side of the bed. He wouldn't have been able to sleep spooned together like this.

I wondered if Beau was worried about me, if he'd even noticed I was missing yet. Probably Fogel had called Tom, and Tom would call Beau. So maybe he was worried. Maybe they were all roaming around the American River looking for me. Not Beau. Beau had his leg in a cast; it would be a long time before he could look for me.

I'd worked myself into despair when Moose finally came in and cut me free of Hammie.

"You should put the dress back on. You'll feel out of place if you wear those jeans again. We need to get you to a laundry."

I grabbed the dress and headed in to take a shower. Just as I reached the door I heard a thump and turned back to see Hammie on the floor.

"Time to get up," Moose said to him.

Hammie took a swipe at Moose's leg, but Moose just moved out of the way. I locked myself in the bathroom and let them sort it out for themselves.

Moose drove us south, out of the city. I don't know why I'd expected us to go east, back toward the Foresthill Bridge, but I had. What was to the south? Stockton, Fresno and points beyond. I dozed in the back seat, which was at least more comfortable than trying to sleep with my legs tied together. Moose pulled off the freeway somewhere between Sacramento and Stockton. We motored along the frontage road for a while before we turned into a gated community.

*It would be hard to escape from here,* I thought as we drove through the iron gates flanked by high cement walls. Very attractive, but as good at keeping people out as they were at keeping them in. The houses were big and set well apart. The landscaping was tasteful and immaculate, if a little sterile for my taste.

"No individuality permitted," I said aloud.

Hammie looked over at me.

"What?"

"It all looks the same," I said, motioning out the window. "No one is allowed to be different."

"What are you talking about? None of those houses look remotely alike. They were all individually designed to spec. Just because they are immaculately groomed doesn't make them identical."

My eyes scanned the houses looking for what Hammie saw in them. "Nope," I said, "can't see it. The houses are different styles, sure, but they're all the same color. They all sit exactly twenty-five feet from the road. I'll bet the same landscaper designed and grooms all of them. It's cookie cutter living. I wouldn't trade my house for any of these."

"Your house is so old, I'm amazed it's still standing. You don't even lock it, but if you did, I still could have gotten in any of the windows."

"I don't normally have to worry about anyone coming in my windows, and the only people who come in through the door are friends and neighbors, except for you. So statistically, I'm justified in leaving my house open. Besides, my dogs keep strangers away. Usually. How did you get past my dogs?" I was appalled. This was the first moment I'd thought of them. Why hadn't they kept Hammie out of the house?

"You didn't poison them did you?" Panic was rising in my throat.

"No, I didn't poison your dogs. I didn't need to. I threw some hamburger into the yard, opened your door, and they ran right to it. They were still gulping it down when I brought you out. The beagle and the big grey dog came over to check you out, but I threw some more meat, and they abandoned you."

My heart sank. Abandoned for a hunk of meat. Why hadn't I trained them not to take meat from strangers? For the same reason I didn't lock my doors. I didn't think it was necessary. There wasn't much in my house worth stealing except me, apparently.

We pulled into the drive of a three-story house with the same brown and beige as the rest of the houses, the same lawn. The garage doors opened, and Moose pulled into one of the bays next to a limo identical to the one we were in. We all got out of the car, and Hammie escorted me into the house. Paris met us in the hall and followed along throwing daggers into my back with her eyes.

We walked through a kitchen big enough to feed the entire state of Vermont and into the living room, cozy compared to the kitchen, but still big enough to host a marching band. The ceiling was three stories high. I liked the windows, though. They rose from floor to ceiling giving a view of the foothills to the west. The back yard was a pool, cement pathways and big ferns.

"Where's the security wall?" I turned to Hammie, but Moose answered.

"It doesn't go all the way around."

I looked at Moose with my eyebrows raised. "What's the point of a gated community if anyone can just waltz right into the back yard?"

"The wall extends a mile beyond the last house at each end," he said, "runs back a couple of hundred feet. There are motion detectors and security cameras so when someone tries to go around, they get picked up and whisked off to jail. One or two crooks tried it when the community first went in. They got maybe fifty feet into the perimeter before they were picked up. Don't think anyone has tried it since then."

Senator Wallace walked into the room, and everyone tensed. He had on tan slacks and a brown golf shirt and carried a worn briefcase. For some reason the briefcase reminded me that I'd been abducted and wasn't here of my own free will. The smile faded from my face.

Wallace sat on one of the soft leather couches and motioned me to sit on the one across from him.

"Richard," he said. "Kindly take Paris for a stroll in the yard. I need to talk to Ms. MacGowan. Mr. Moore, get the car ready."

Paris made a face but didn't protest when Hammie led her out the door. Moose disappeared back down the hall towards the garage as Wallace set the briefcase on the coffee table between us and extracted two photos from it. He set the photos on the table and used two fingers to slide them across to me.

"These are the two men who are responsible for my wife's death. Do you recognize them?"

"Your wife's death?"

"The woman you saw fall to her death from the Foresthill Bridge. She was my wife."

"Your wife." I fell silent. I didn't want to push the innocence factor too much. I didn't know exactly how much he knew.

The photos were five-by-seven head shots taken in black and white. A round-faced bald man with dark eyebrows stared at me from the first photo. The second had a thin face, dark, stringy, shoulder length hair and light eyes. I shook my head. Neither man was familiar to me.

"I didn't see anything, Senator."

"And your camera?"

He knew about my camera. If I hadn't been sitting in front of him, I would have slapped myself on the head. Of course he knew. He probably sent the guys who broke into the cabin and car. I looked Senator Wallace in the eyes.

"If my camera picked up anything, I never saw it. The sheriff's department took my memory card. I lost all the photos I had of my time in California."

The Senator leaned into me, making me extremely uncomfortable.

"Bree, it's very important that the people responsible for the death of my wife are brought to justice. I don't think I can achieve that without your help. As far as we know you were the only eye witness."

*Besides the thugs who were with you and the suit in the woods. Too bad the bear can't testify.*

"Isn't it the Sheriff's job to bring these guys to justice?" I slid the photos back across the table.

"Sheriff Fogel is out of his league. I'm doing all I can to help him." He smiled and pushed the photos back to me. "Take another look," he said, "just in case."

"They don't ring any bells." I looked briefly, then picked up the pictures and handed them to him. His glance dropped, and I realized that he was looking down my dress. My face flushed, and I stood and turned to look out the window. Hammie and Paris were sitting by the pool. He was leaning into her, talking earnestly. She had turned away and was looking out into the hills. I felt sorry for him. She was obviously cold and calculating, and he deserved better.

"Bree." The senator's voice was close behind me. "You'd be doing a good thing, identifying these men. I know pulling Lily from the river must have been very traumatic for you. This would be a way to make it better."

I turned to face him. "Lying will not make me feel better. I'd like to help, but I can't." *You probably killed her and I won't lie to get you off the hook.* "Sheriff Fogel sent me home because I didn't see anything except a body in the river. If he thought I'd be any help, he would have kept me here. I want to go back home now. My family will be worried about me."

"Your animals are being well taken care of, and your family knows that you are here as my guest. No one is looking for you." His voice was smooth, but the lack of menace gave me chills. He expected to get what he wanted, and if he didn't, I'd end up falling from the Foresthill Bridge with a bullet in my head.

I turned back to the windows as he motioned Paris and Hammie back into the room. I'd rather Hammie see the distress on my face than Senator Wallace. As it was, Paris glanced at my face as they entered the room, but Hammie kept his face turned away from me.

"Paris, come sit and amuse me, dear. Richard, please show Ms. MacGowan to her room."

It was a pleasant enough room with pale yellow walls and an attached bathroom, but I couldn't wait to get out of it. I'd been in a lot of crummy situations in the last six months or so, and I was ready for a change of pace that didn't include dead bodies, being drugged or abducted. I missed my friends, my animals and Beau, of course. I hoped he was taking it easy, not that he had any alternative. It's kind of difficult to get yourself into trouble when you've got your leg in a cast.

I stood at the window looking out over the gold and green landscape. It hadn't rained enough to turn the hills completely green, but you could see it coming in patches. California was so strange compared to Vermont where it was green and lush in the summer, brown and muddy in November and April, and barren and snow-covered the rest of the year. Here, brown was still the prominent color, but I could see that given a couple of good rains the hills would be green again. Green in the winter, go figure.

There was a quiet knock, and Paris let herself in the room. She plopped onto the bed. I half expected her to collapse backward and let the bed support her, but she kept her spine straight and scowled at me.

"Wallace sent me in here to talk you into identifying the guys that murdered his wife. Thought maybe a woman's touch would soften you up. Personally, I don't think you're that gullible."

My emotions were near breaking point again, and I didn't want to go crazy on this girl like I had on Hammie last night. I turned to the window again, gazing out across the fields. If I went out the window at night, how far could I get before someone caught up with me? Paris moved restlessly behind me, and I turned back to her.

"Do you know anything about what happened?" I asked.

"Only rumors. They're flying thick and fast. Half the people I talk to are convinced that Wallace killed his own wife, the other half think someone had it out for her for other reasons. I don't know what's true." She flopped back onto the bed. "I wish Richard would get the heck out of here. Wallace gives me the creeps, and now I'm stuck here, too, unless we can get you to cave." She turned her head and looked at me. "You're not going to cave, are you?"

"Don't think so."

"He'll find a way. Richard didn't want to work for him. Told him flat out no. And look where he is now."

"Why would the senator want someone working for him who didn't want to be there? Doesn't make sense."

"Because Richard's the best at what he does. He's an ex-Navy Seal. Got all kinds of awards. Could probably get in the FBI or the CIA if he wanted, but he doesn't want that. He wants to put all that stuff behind him and be a normal person now."

Paris seemed too naive to be with a guy like Hammie, but maybe that's what he wanted, someone who couldn't imagine or guess what he'd done. Someone who would comfort him when he woke up in a cold sweat but wouldn't ask questions.

"How did you meet Ham, er, Richard?"

She smiled and stared at the ceiling, stretching her arms up over her head and wiggling into the comforter.

"He's a friend of my older brother. They were in the Navy together, and when Roger got out he brought Richard home. We've been dating ever since. He won't even sleep with me," she closed her eyes, "because I'm Roger's sister. Says I should wait until I'm married. It was really nice until Senator Gets-What-He-Wants got his hooks into Richard. That spoiled everything. I know it's not your fault he had to sit with you at the concert, but it's awful that Richard is spending all his time doing stuff for him. It's not fair."

"Yeah? Well, life's not fair. At least that's what my momma always told me. So what are you going to tell Senator Gets-What-He-Wants about me?"

"Oh, I don't know. I think I'll hang out in here a while longer. He won't bug me while I'm in with you. He kind of gives me the creeps, and he never leaves me alone with Richard anymore. Richard's noticed it too. He was mad when I wore that red coat. Wallace gave it to me, and Richard said I should give it back. He doesn't want me to be indebted to Wallace. I like the coat. I'm not giving it back."

"It's your decision."

I turned back to the window and examined how it opened. It was one of those sliding jobbies, the kind that opens by sliding to the side instead of up and down. It wasn't locked. A ground floor room with a locked door but unlocked windows. A mixture of emotion spread through me. The sane part of my brain was sending out warning signals, the other was planning my escape.

"They locked me in here but didn't bother to lock the windows."

"There's some sort of perimeter alarm. They don't need to lock the windows or the rear doors because a siren goes off if anyone goes through the back yard. There's a motion detector on the property line."

I went back to planning my escape anyway. Maybe if I jumped off the roof I could avoid setting off the alarm. Then I remembered the roof was three stories high.

"Damn!"

Paris jumped up, and I realized I'd spoken out loud.

"Sorry, didn't mean to startle you." I hadn't noticed that she'd gone to sleep.

"S'okay." Paris rubbed her eyes. "I shouldn't be sleeping now anyway. I'm getting into a bad cycle. I can't sleep at night, and I end up napping during the day. Then I can't sleep at night. It's the awful hours here. They get you all strung out so you'll be confused and easily manipulated. Richard told me that."

*Smart Richard*, I thought. I went back to scanning the back yard and the hills beyond. After all, this place wasn't built as a fortress, so there had to be ways to get in and out without detection. I heard Paris get up off the bed and turned to see her pulling her clothes back into place.

"I'm going to my room," she said. "Maybe he won't find me for a while."

"Hang on."

"Yeah?" She turned to look at me, her hand on the doorknob.

"Why are you staying here? Couldn't you go home if you wanted?"

"I'm not sure if they'd let me go home or not, but if I did leave, I'm pretty sure I'd never see Richard again. It's up to me to save him."

*Great, another woman who thinks she needs to rescue her man.* I shook my head as Paris slid out of the room and waited to hear the lock click back into place. It didn't. I crossed to the door and tried the handle. It turned. I waited until Paris had plenty of time to get up the stairs, cracked the door open and looked up and down the empty hall. I slipped off the blue heels and ran silently down the hall past several closed doors in my bare feet. The carpet muffled any sound my feet may have made and I reached the wide stairs at the end of the hall before my brain kicked in and I started to have doubts.

But the doubts died a quick and painless death because there, across a vaulted and sun-lit foyer, was the entrance door. Not the door through the garage that I came in through, but the front door. The door to freedom. I'd started across the tile, thinking of freedom and not what I'd do once I was out that door, when a hand covered my mouth and an arm caught me around the waist. *Hammie*, I thought as he dragged me backward into the hall I'd just come down. Who else would be man-handling me? Sure enough, when the arm around my waist relaxed, I spun around to find Hammie, finger to his lips. His arm was still around my waist, and he was too close for comfort. I struggled to break free.

"Stop it!" he hissed in my ear. "I need to talk to you." He dragged me through one of the doors lining the hallway into a small room. Books lined the walls, two overstuffed armchairs flanked a small round table, and the same floor-to-ceiling windows as the living room let light into the room. A small desk sat facing the view of the pool.

Hambecker released his hold on me, and I almost fell into one of the comfy chairs.

"What the hell do you think you're doing, trying to get yourself killed?" he asked.

"Nice room," I said. It was a nice room, but I didn't want Wallace to have nice rooms. "How did you know I snuck out?"

"Your room is bugged, and there are cameras in the hallway. When Moose isn't driving, his job is to watch the video feed from the cameras."

"Guess that explains why the senator needs more than one driver. I suppose you're going to lock me back in and pump me full of knock-out drugs again now." I fought an irrational urge to stomp my foot. I wanted to at least pretend I was mature and in control of the situation.

"Every time I think I'm going to get away, you're one step behind me, and since you're faster than me, it's just as good as being one step ahead. Do you have any idea how annoying that is?"

"Bree, I need to talk to you. I need you to play along with Senator Wallace for a while. Whatever it is he wants you to do, pretend that you'll do it. Give me some time."

"It's illegal."

"It's not illegal if you stay of your own free will."

"Not that, what he's asking me to do. It's against the law."

"I didn't say you should do it. Pretend. Go along with him so I can find out what I need to know. I can't be spending all my time chasing you down. I don't want to have to handcuff you to the bed, but I will if that's what it takes to keep you in one place."

I could understand his dilemma, but I wasn't telling him that. I didn't want to be another Patty Hearst, no matter how attractive and sympathetic I found Hammie. And Moose was just like a big teddy bear. How these guys got mixed up with a slimeball like Wallace, I didn't know. I did know I'd have to keep my wits about me not to get pulled into their drama. I had my own life to worry about.

"Yeah, I know. I kidnapped you, drugged you, flew you three thousand miles from home. All bad stuff. But I promise, I'll help you get home if you'll just give me some time. Tell Wallace you'll do what he asked. Just keep him focused on you, and I'll get you home."

"And if I don't?" I got up and walked to the little desk by the window, keeping my back to Hammie.

"I'll chain you to the shower curtain rod in your bathroom."

"Nice." I dropped my gaze to examine the top of the desk. Note paper, stapler, pens, paper clips. Paper clips?

"Not nice. Desperate enough to do whatever it takes."

I closed my eyes. What choice did I have? My best bet was to remain unchained. I realized I was going about this the wrong way, I should be agreeing to anything and everything Hammie or Wallace wanted. Sooner or later that would involve telling the cops a lie, unless I told them the truth. Bait and switch, wasn't that what it was called? I opened my eyes.

"Okay. I'll cooperate, but if anything bad happens to my animals while I'm away, I'm holding you responsible. I will hunt you down." I turned and looked him in the eye, palming a paper clip.

Hammie snorted, and a flash of humor animated his face before he closed back down again. He was amused by my threats. Good. I didn't want him to take me too seriously.

Hambecker took me back down the hall to my room. I turned, moving toward the little desk on the other side of the room, thinking I had plans to make, but I came to a dead stop. I wasn't alone.

# Seven

Senator Wallace was lying spread-eagled on my bed. He opened his eyes as the lock clicked. I backed against the wall and pretended that I wasn't scared out of my wits.

"Ah, there you are. Did Richard take you for a tour of the house?"

My stomach started to churn, and I had the uncomfortable feeling he was testing me. Every muscle was tense, and I fought the urge to throw up.

"No."

"Good girl. I'm glad you didn't lie. Of course he caught you trying to leave. Silly Paris forgot to lock your door, didn't she?"

I wondered if he had asked Paris to leave the door unlocked. The paper clip that I had hidden between two of my fingers was poking into my hand. I fought the urge to drop it.

"Not that I blame you for trying to leave. Richard tells me you aren't exactly a willing guest. Not his fault, I told him to do whatever it took to get you here. Richard is very good at doing what I tell him." Wallace pushed himself up and sat on the edge of the bed.

"I'm going to San Francisco to visit my daughter for a couple of days. I'm leaving you here with Richard and my driver. They'll make sure you are fed and watered while I'm gone. Be nice to them, and they'll be nice to you. I've given them permission to lock you in with no meals if you give them trouble. Understand?"

I nodded again. I wasn't unhappy that he was going to be away.

Wallace stood and walked over to me. He placed his hands on my shoulders, and I resisted the urge to shudder and shove him away from me.

"I want you to think hard about what I asked you to do and the good you would be doing for society as a whole. I'll talk to you when I come back."

I nodded. He released me and walked to the door.

"Feel free to enjoy the pool while I'm gone. You can go anywhere you'd like as long as it's not out the front door." The door closed behind him, and I waited for the lock to click, but it didn't. He was giving me free reign of the house. That was interesting. Trying to soften me up, make me comfortable. Make me like him. The knot in my gut made me pretty sure I was never going to like him. I don't know what he was trying to accomplish by putting his hands on me unless it was a subtle form of intimidation. I placed the paper clip in the toe of one of the blue shoes. You never knew when you might need a paper clip.

I left my room and made my way through the foyer into the kitchen. I stood at the sink where I could pretend to be getting a drink of water while I waited for the limo to disappear down the street. I wondered if Moose was driving or if he'd been left here. I knew Wallace had more than one driver. What I didn't know is which one he had left to guard me. Moose, I could handle.

I gave Wallace time to get out the main gate before I started to snoop. Hammie was going to be a problem, so I crept along quietly going from room to room looking for something of interest. The ground floor was dedicated to entertaining and bedrooms. I wandered in and out of the living room, a TV room with a giant flat screen on the wall and theatre seating for twenty. A game room was situated across from the garage; there was a door at the end, which led to a cabana house with changing room and sauna. Nothing of interest.

I was back in the game room. I'd racked the balls and taken a couple of shots at the pool table when Hammie came in. Perfect timing. I kept my smile to myself and raised my eyebrows at him.

"Want to play pool or foosball? Wallace knows how to throw a party."

"What are you doing?" Hammie was frowning at me.

"The senator gave me free reign of the house. I was looking for something to do. It's pretty quiet around here. Where's Paris? Maybe she'd play foosball with me."

"Paris is Wendy's best friend. She went with him to San Francisco."

Better and better. That meant fewer people to keep an eye on me. I looked up into Hammie's scowl with my eyes wide.

"Is the pool heated?"

"Yes." His tone was guarded.

"Do you think Paris has a bathing suit that would fit me? I'd love to go for a swim."

"Not sure. You can't swim now anyway. I need to do some errands. I'm locking you in while I'm away."

"Senator Wallace said I could have the run of the house. Can't you just lock the house up?"

"No. I'm leaving Moose here with you. You'll be locked in until I get back."

He wasn't going to tell me that I could convince Moose to do just about anything, but I knew that was why he was going to lock me in. He didn't trust Moose not to take me to the shopping center for a swimsuit and lose me there.

I followed Hammie down the hall and stepped into my room.

"Don't be long," I said, and smiled my sweetest at him.

He shook his head as he closed the door. The lock snapped, and I got the feeling he didn't trust himself to say anything. I felt sorry for Hammie. It seemed like he was in a tight spot, but I had to remember that he was one of the enemy camp. As far as I knew, he and Moose were feeding me a line of crap about Hambecker's father to keep me in line.

I waited until I imagined I heard an engine start in the garage, and then I pulled the paper clip out of the shoe and straightened it. Ten seconds of wiggling the clip in the tiny hole in the door handle, and the lock clicked open.

I cracked the door, stuck my head out, and looked up and down the hall. All clear. Good. I reached around the door and pushed the little button in the outer handle and locked myself back in the room. I might as well sleep now, as my plan was to search the house at night, while Hammie and Moose were sleeping.

It was dusk when the door opened, and Moose brought in a tray of food. I thought of refusing it out of principle, but it smelled good. Somehow I'd missed breakfast and lunch, and the sight of food reminded me I was hungry.

"Richard says I can't let you out to eat. Thinks I'm a soft touch or something." He rolled his eyes. "Like it would hurt anything for you to go swimming. Anywho, here's your dinner. Hope you like it."

It was a burger and fries, Caesar salad and chocolate chip cookies.

"Looks fabulous," I said. I stuffed a couple of French fries in my mouth. "Yum. Why don't you sit down and keep me company?"

"Can't." Moose looked uncomfortable. "He made me promise not to stay with you too long."

"He who? Wallace or Hammie?"

"Ham, er, Richard." He dropped his head and looked at his feet, looking for all the world like a five-year-old who'd been caught with his grandma's cigarettes, which was pretty amazing when you considered how big this guy was.

"I'll go get you something to drink. You can have soda, water or juice. We have beer, but Richard said you can't have any."

"That's okay, Moose. Something with caffeine would be nice."

Moose left, and I noticed that he forgot to lock the door. I was too busy eating to bother with getting out. Besides, I had plans for later. He was back in a minute anyway with a glass of ice and a couple of sodas, "In case you get thirsty later," and he left, remembering to lock the door this time.

The room was dark when I opened my eyes. There wasn't a clock in the room, my cell phone was on the opposite side of the country, and I didn't wear a watch. I rolled out of bed and looked out the window. Light from the direction of the living room was reflecting on the pool. I pressed my ear to the window. Faint sounds of TV? I went to the door and tried the handle. Still locked. I pressed my ear to the wood, definite TV sounds. Hammie, Moose or both were still awake. I plopped back down on the bed to wait them out.

My neck hurt, not as bad as it had been, but I wasn't in the best shape ever. Better remember to ask Hammie for some pain killer, ib-whatever. Why they couldn't make medicines pronounceable, I had no idea. Or he could hit me with more of that knockout drug, whatever that was. That took care of the pain really well.

I woke to the vague feeling that something wasn't right. A faint light filled the room. "Damn!" I sat bolt upright. I'd slept the night in the blue dress on top of the bed, and I'd missed my opportunity to search the house. Probably. The light from the window was pretty faint. Maybe there was enough time for a preliminary search of the upper floors.

The blue shoes were sitting next to the bed where I'd abandoned them the day before. I grabbed them and dumped the paper clip into my hand. Carrying my shoes with my left hand, I stuck the straight end into the hole in the door handle. A minute later the lock clicked and I was free. Cracking the door, I stuck my head into the hall and listened. Nothing. I slid out of the door and locked it behind me. If anyone walked by, they would assume I was still in there.

The stairs at the end of the hall felt uncomfortably open, but if I wanted to search the upper floors I'd have no choice but to go up them. The polished wood was smooth and cool under my feet. I stepped lightly, but there weren't any creaky stairs. This house was built like a rock.

Halfway up I heard a toilet flush. Sweat prickled on my scalp, and I stood frozen against the wall. There were footsteps in the hall, and a door closed. I moved as quickly and quietly as I could past the second floor and on up to the third. I turned to the right, my thinking being that most people preferred the right, and if Wallace's office was up here it would be that direction.

The first three doors revealed nothing but beds and storage rooms. This guy could host the Sacramento Kings and have room left over. The other side of the hall wasn't any better, except that from the windows I could see out onto the road. Wallace had the tallest house in the area so the neighborhood unfolded in front of me. Nothing and no one in sight except for a car parked around the corner to the left. The only car left on the street overnight. Someone's girlfriend?

I searched the rest of the rooms on the third floor without finding anything remotely interesting. There was an office of sorts, but it was dusty and unused. The late Lily Wallace's? It looked like a woman's office, colorful prints on the wall, small desk and chair, a painted tile for a coaster. I searched through the drawers without finding anything. The senator had probably been cleaning it out while someone was tossing her off the bridge.

The only place left was the second floor. Creeping down the stairs I considered leaving it for the night, but it was quiet. My main problem was figuring out which rooms were occupied so I didn't wake anyone up by mistake.

The first door was easy. I could hear the snores from the top of the stairs. Moose. I'd heard him snoring in the hotel. I did my best imitation of a ghost past his door, the carpet doing a good job of muffling my footsteps. My heart started thumping at the second door. My hand was on the knob, ready to crack the door open, when a faint rustling and a creak sent me down the hall and into the next room. It was a gamble, but I won. The room was empty.

I stood at the door, listening until the door to the room next to me opened and shut and I heard footsteps on the stairway. I waited for what seemed like forever, but it was probably less than five minutes before I ventured out into the hall again. I had a hunch about the layout and hurried past the stairs to a door at the end of the hall. I hit the jackpot. A mahogany desk, file cabinets, bookshelves signaled that I'd found the senator's office.

I started through the desk drawers. No papers, but I pulled out a ring of keys triumphantly. I'd bet my life they were to the filing cabinets. My hands were shaking when I got the files open. I rifled through the top drawer, going through all the files because I didn't trust the labels. I doubted he'd file anything under Wife's Murder or Foiled Divorce, so I had to look through everything.

It was hard to know what was important, so I was reading a lot of stuff I didn't understand. The top drawer was a bust, and I moved on to the middle. Time was ticking away. The longer I spent in here, the more likely I'd be caught. And what was I going to say? I was curious?

I was on my knees, well into the third drawer when the door opened behind me.

"Shit." I jumped up, bumping my knee on the corner of the drawer and bringing tears to my eyes. I pushed the drawer shut and turned to find Hammie standing inside the door, arms crossed, watching me.

"Did Senator Wallace give you permission to search his office?" He had the daddy-caught-you-misbehaving look on his face. *Bastard. Stop patronizing me.*

"Could you be any more sarcastic? The Senator told me I had free reign of the house. Said I could go anywhere."

"You took that to mean you could search his office?"

*You damn well know I'm not supposed to be searching his office so don't ask stupid questions.*

"I'm surprised you're not searching his office. You're the one compromising your principles to protect your father." *Don't kid yourself, Bree. He's not exactly superman. He'd be riding the edge of the law even if his father was squeaky clean.*

"You don't know that I haven't searched this office. In fact, you don't know much of anything, it seems to me. A total waste of my time and the senator's." This was a Hammie I'd never seen before. His face was set, emotions shut down. I'd made him angry. Well, good.

"Since when do you care about the senator's time?" I was getting pretty steamed myself. I figured I had as many facts as Hammie did.

"Since he's my boss."

"Then I suppose you know that your boss most likely had his wife killed." I watched his face, but he'd shut down good. He was making damn sure he wasn't giving anything away.

"That's the stupidest thing I've ever heard. She loved power, she wouldn't have divorced him."

"Oh, really, a lot you know about women. Lily was the money and the power behind the senator." I knew she had the money, but I was guessing on the power thing.

Anyway it sounded good, and for some reason I wanted to win this argument.

"She had the money," I went on, "then she disappeared. When she reappeared she had a bullet in her head, and now Wallace has the money."

"How do you come up with this shit?" He was leaning against the door now, looking at me with contempt.

"I happened to pull her body out of the river, which is why Senator Wallace sent you after me. He's trying to clear himself by asking me to implicate some innocent criminals. Told me I'd be doing society a service. He's a toad."

"In your opinion."

"Yes, in my opinion he's a toad. I was drugged, kidnapped from my home, flown all the way across the country against my will. I'm being held indefinitely while my family and friends worry. He's not just a toad. He's a fucking toad. I want to go home."

"I just need a little more time."

"I don't understand you. Wallace has your dad over a barrel, but you refuse to believe that he's capable of murdering his wife. It's all part of the same immorality."

"Blackmail and murder are two different things."

"Take off the effing blinders. Jeez. I can't deal with you." I picked up my shoes and pushed past him. I didn't have a thing that would link Wallace to Lily's murder, but only a fool would keep that kind of evidence around. Hambecker didn't follow me from the room. As I came down the stairs the foyer and entry were beckoning me. I increased my speed down the stairs, listening for Hammie to come after me. He wasn't. I reached the first floor, the foyer tile cold and smooth beneath my feet. I sprinted toward freedom.

I was out the door, flying down the front walk in my bare feet. The skirt of the blue dress kept wrapping around my legs, so I hitched it up with the hand that wasn't carrying the impractical shoes. I thought briefly about chucking the shoes, but you never know when you might need a good pair of heels, so I held onto them. I was telling myself I needed the shoes for when I approached a house, but in reality I'd never had shoes that matched a dress and I didn't want to dump them.

I ran out into the street and looked both ways. I couldn't see far in either direction because of the turns and little hills that were engineered into the road. I cursed the idiot who designed it. I imagined the road crew that had to pave this shaking their heads at the stupidity. Sacramento County was flat, open land. Roadways were flat and straight too, but not this one. My natural tendency was to go to the right, so I gritted my teeth and ran to the left.

The car I'd seen parked by the side of the road from the second story window sat around the first bend. I slowed to a walk and stepped up onto a lawn. There were no sidewalks. The developer didn't expect the residents would want to walk anywhere, or perhaps he thought they would just walk in the road. After all, there wasn't really any traffic here.

I kept my eyes trained on the car as I approached. No one parked on the street in this community. No one. The driver was motionless. Sitting in the car, a pink sweatshirt hood covering the head propped on the steering wheel. *Just what I need, another dead body. I'm not stopping, I don't care, someone else can find her.* I started to trot again. I moved past the car, and my shadow fell on the driver's side window. The head jerked up off the steering wheel, startled blue eyes staring at me. She screamed. I screamed and jumped back so fast I tripped and landed on my ass in the grass. My heart stopped pumping, and I thought, *I'm going to die right here on someone's front lawn.*

The terror on the driver's face morphed into surprise, and she reached back and popped the back door open and started the car.

"Come on!" She hissed and she flicked the hood off her head, revealing lavender hair pulled into a ponytail. "You think they are going to wait all day before they come looking for you?"

She didn't have to ask twice. I dived into the back seat and slammed the door. I expected her to turn the car and drive away from the Senator's house, but she headed back toward it.

"No! No! Go the other way."

"Can't. There's only one way out of this place, and it's right past Senator Wallace. It's the only reason I could stay parked on the street back there. Wallace has the last inhabited house. No one drives past here."

We rounded the corner, and I flattened myself to the back seat, praying we'd get past. When the car didn't come to a screeching halt, I sat back up. I looked at the side of the driver's face, and it dawned on me that I'd seen her before.

"You're the crazy shape-shifting alien woman," I said.

"Yep, that's me."

"You followed me from Vermont? That's a little strange."

"Strange? I'm a shape-shifting alien, and you think it's strange that I followed you?"

"I don't actually think you shape shift, you know."

"But it's possible I'm an alien."

"Doubtful." I pulled on the seat belt.

She handed me a knit cap and an army jacket. "Put those on. We should be able to get out of the gate easily enough, but if someone approaches us, you are my teenage son."

*Great. I get to be a teenaged boy now.* I pulled the cap over my head and tucked up my hair in the back. The jacket smelled of body odor and cigarette smoke, but I unbuckled and pulled it on anyway. I could shower later. If anyone took a good look in the car I was screwed, the blue dress hung out from underneath the jacket. I'd make a very strange boy.

I held my breath as she punched the code into the pad, and the gate rolled back. We had rolled through the gate and out onto the road when her cell phone began to ring.

"I'm busy, Hambecker, what do you want? Yeah, I have her. No, you can't have her back." The phone flipped closed.

I closed my mouth

"I'm confused," I said. "That was Hammie?"

"You call *Hambecker* Hammie?" Her smile widened. "To his face?"

"So?"

"Really? To his face?" She laughed out loud. "Oh, my God, I am *so* doing that."

She drove onto the freeway and headed north, back toward Sacramento proper.

"If you don't mind my asking, who are you?" I tugged off the foul-smelling coat and hat.

"Agent Madison Truefellow, abducted female rescuer. I'm far better at it than Hambecker, although to give him credit his objectives are different than mine."

"As far as I can tell he's a female abductor, not a rescuer at all. What are your objectives?" I wasn't sure I wanted to know. I was driving along with a gleeful, self-proclaimed alien shape-shifting, what? FBI agent? She hadn't shown me a badge or anything, and although I was glad to be away from the grasping senator, I was pretty sure I was the only one who had my best interests at heart.

"I'm supposed to keep you safe until the whole Lily Carver Wallace thing has been solved. I have to say I thought it would be a hell of a lot easier than it is. I nearly shit my pants when you disappeared. I figured you were pretty safe as long as you were holed up at home."

"Are you telling me that Hammie is a Fed?"

"Richard Hambecker has divided loyalties, and I don't trust him. His number one priority is known only to himself and maybe to his boss, although I have to say having him in the senator's camp has been incredibly useful."

"Wait, I thought Hammie was an ex-Navy Seal. Are you telling me he's a special agent?"

"Oh, he was a Navy Seal all right. Came right out of the service and got attached to Wallace. Not sure *who* he's working for or if the whole thing with his dad is real or not. What I do know is that Hambecker Sr. is as straight as they get, but the whole blackmail thing gives Hambecker Jr. a reason to be less than squeaky clean."

"Which is good for his standing with the senator, which gives Hammie more access to what's going on."

"You got it."

"So how come you didn't know he was going to come get me? Shouldn't you two be communicating?"

"I'm not positive we are on the same side. I'd say we're probably on the same side but with different objectives. He hasn't really had much to say since he's been in the senator's camp." Madison looked over at me. "How long has it been since you've eaten?"

"I'm not sure. I think I ate something yesterday."

We took the next exit, and she pulled into the drive through at a fast food place. Three bites into a breakfast sandwich, grease dripped out the bottom of the wrapper and landed on my chest. I looked down at the blue dress. It was a little worse for wear. It was wrinkled, and the greasy smear was sitting next to what looked like a toothpaste stain.

"Do you think we could stop somewhere and get me some clothes? I've been wearing this dress for ages. It stinks. Literally."

"I shouldn't take the time," Madison looked at the dress, "but I wouldn't want to be stuck in that dress. It'll be a while before we get this chance again."

Thank God I was with Madison. I can't imagine Hammie understanding my need for clean clothes and comfortable shoes. I pulled the blue shoes onto my feet as we pulled into the mall across from the burger joint.

An hour later we came out through the big mall entry. I was wearing jeans, a white, girl-cut long-sleeve tee, clean undies, socks and bra, and sneakers courtesy of the FBI. At least I think it was the FBI. I wasn't sure Madison had ever really cleared that up. I was carrying a new jacket, still in the bag, in case it got cold. The blue dress and shoes were in a bag under my other arm. We'd picked up some stain stick and treated the fresh stain, hoping that it would come out when we finally got the dress cleaned.

Madison was striding along ahead of me, leading me back to the car, when I noticed her hair looked like it was changing color again. The ends were starting to look a little pink. I was trying to convince myself I was seeing things, which is why I walked right into her when she stopped.

"Oh, shit," Madison said and stared at her car. I followed her gaze.

Richard Hambecker was leaning against the driver side door, arms crossed, eyebrows raised.

# Eight

"Oh, hell no." For the first time since I'd met her on the plane, Madison had her cop face on.

"Come on, Maddy, I need Bree."

"She's been at Wallace's long enough, Richard. It's time to get her out of there."

"If she escapes, Wallace may decide he no longer needs me."

"You've been too valuable to him. He may be mad, but he won't cut you loose. You were too hard to get in the first place."

"I'm taking her." Hammie pushed himself up off the side of the car.

"No, you're not." Madison pushed me behind her.

"Um, don't you guys have a superior officer who could settle this?" I was throwing my lot in with the anonymous boss, who might at least be following the rules. Hopefully, the rules said something about the kidnapped witness getting her life back.

"No." They spoke together, united against me now. It came to me in a flash that they might not be on the same team, but I wasn't even in the same league. Whatever their prime objectives were, it wasn't about getting me home.

"I need to take her in," Madison said.

"You don't need to do that. Leave her with me, call your boss, tell him where she is and what you know so far. He can act on that information."

"Is the boss FBI? Because I was kidnapped and transported across state lines."

"You weren't actually kidnapped. You were relocated for your own protection."

"Relocated? I was knocked unconscious for almost twenty-four hours."

Madison and Hammie exchanged glances. I could see them realigning allegiances. *Think, Bree, who's the only one who isn't a cop?* I turned and ran.

I had about a three-second start. I sprinted to the mall, yanked open the huge glass door, and ran for the largest department store in the place. The only trouble was that the largest store was also the farthest away. I risked a glance over my shoulder. No one was following me. I stopped in my tracks. Why wouldn't they be chasing me? I jogged past shops, glancing over my shoulder every couple of seconds. They didn't appear.

I sat on a bench, the bag with the blue dress in my lap. What possible reason could they have for not following me? I wasn't that important? That I could believe. I didn't really know anything. Hammie was right earlier when he said I was a waste of time. Other than the pictures Fogel had taken off my camera I was a no-go as a witness. I hadn't seen anything except blurry images in a photograph.

The problem was that I was now on my own, which was good, except I didn't have any ID, money, or transportation. I toyed with stealing Madison's car. She wouldn't be stranded, because Hammie could give her a ride. *How could I manage it?* I set the thought aside as too risky. I'd need the keys and didn't want to get close enough to whatever kind of agents they were to get them.

I leaned my elbows on my knees and dropped my head in my hands. It wasn't an impossible situation, was it? I got up off the bench and walked aimlessly down the mall, away from the doors I'd come in.

My neck was throbbing. The physical therapist wasn't going to be happy with me. Everything I'd done since injuring it was guaranteed to aggravate it. I looked around me for a store that carried one of those electric chair massagers. The thought of sinking into a chair and letting the heat and vibration lull me to sleep was overwhelming. Tears pricked the backs of my eyes, but I blinked them back. Time to get proactive.

As much as I loved the new jacket, it was the one thing I had that I could exchange for money. I picked up the pace and power-walked down the mall to the store where we'd bought the coat. Madison had paid cash for my stuff, and while she'd pocketed the receipt for the other stuff, she'd been distracted when we'd paid for the jacket, and the clerk had put the receipt in the bag.

I avoided the clerk who had waited on us and walked to the customer service counter at the back of the store. The clerk took the jacket, and I got Madison's money. *Well, it's really the FBI's money, which is funded by my taxes, so it's my money. Right?* I went in search of a pay phone.

As I left the store I heard someone call out to me.

"Yes?" I turned to see the young man who had taken the coat.

"You forgot your lipstick. It dropped out of your other bag." He handed me a bullet-shaped tube, silver with a passion pink lid.

"Not mine." I frowned and tried to hand it back to him.

"No. It's yours. I saw it fall out of the bag you're carrying."

I didn't even wear lipstick. I shoved the thing in my pocket and focused on finding a phone.

I looked for the public restrooms and hit the jackpot. The trouble was that it was the kind of pay phone that required a calling card to call long distance. Great.

I walked back down the mall until I found a Walgreens, where I bought a long distance card from the check out and waited while they activated it. I turned to go back to the phone bank and nearly ran smack into the back of Hammie and Madison. They were facing away from me, still arguing. I backed away, turned and ran. I took the escalator stairs two at a time and looked over the railing to check on them. They were walking down to the lower level looking at something Hammie held in his hand.

I backed away from the rail and jogged down to the upper floor restrooms, also sporting a bank of phones. But no phone books. I dialed information and got the number for the Placer County Sheriff's Department. I was punching in the number when I caught a glimpse of pink from the corner of my eye as Madison came around the corner. I dropped the phone and hightailed it out the opposite end of the bathroom corridor. I turned right, spotted Hammie coming, did a quick u-turn and ran smack into Moose's arms.

"Crap, crap, crap." I struggled to get free of Moose's embrace, but I wasn't strong enough. I went to stomp on

Moose's instep, but he lifted me off the ground, effectively disarming me.

Madison appeared beside us, reached into her handbag and pulled out a set of metal cuffs, one of which she slapped on my wrist. She went to put the other on her wrist, but Hammie reached out to stop her.

"Cuff her to me. You're not heavy enough to control her if she gets out of hand."

"I've got a gun. She won't get out of hand." She clicked the cuff on her wrist.

"Gosh," I said. "Madison must be a real cop. She's got real metal cuffs and a gun. She's not using those *el cheapo* nylon things."

"I've got nylon cuffs, I just think it's easier to cuff two people together with metal ones."

I contemplated throwing a fit and causing a scene but discarded it as an option because it was probably fruitless. Madison had me out-gunned and out-badged, and it wasn't likely that anyone would take me seriously. I didn't know what Moose or Hammie had, but it didn't matter. I was screwed.

"Come on." Madison tugged on the cuff, and Moose released me to the ground. I wanted to kick him in the ankle, but he'd been nice to me before, so I didn't. We walked three abreast with me in the middle and Hammie right behind me.

"Is Moose FBI, too?"

"Moose and Hambecker go way back. They're practically joined at the hip. Were in the service together. May even have gone to high school together. Wallace hired Moose as a driver on Richard's recommendation."

"I don't understand why Hammie pulled me off that plane like a fugitive when he could have just explained the situation to Fogel. What was that all about?"

"Would you stop talking about me like I'm not here? I didn't want to blow my cover. Did you notice that no one made a serious attempt to go after you? There were people in the know at a higher level."

"Seems theatrical," I said.

"Hambecker has a penchant for dramatics. It suits his personality."

"Humph."

They walked me back to where we'd left the car.

"We'll stay here," Hambecker said. "Moose, go get the limo."

Moose jogged away down the row of cars, and Hammie faced Madison again.

"I need to take her back to Wallace. He trusts me. If Ms. MacGowan is gone when he gets back I'll have lost my effectiveness."

"She's not safe with Wallace. What if he decides she's a liability and puts a bullet in her head like he did Lily?"

"Ms. MacGowan was out in public with the Senator, so he won't risk killing her. First his wife and then some woman he was seen with are found shot to death? The publicity would kill his career."

"Which is the thing he's trying to save." Madison furrowed her eyebrows. "I still don't like it. She's my assignment, and I can't keep an eye on her if she's at Wallace's place."

"Moose and I can both keep an eye on her there."

"But not as your primary objective. Your attention will be on your assignment, not mine."

"There are two of us, and I thought we'd already established that she'll be safer there than not."

Madison relented and uncuffed me.

Moose pulled the limo alongside of us, and I got in the back, silently cursing the FBI and any other covert agency I could think of.

The trip back to the house was short. We parked in the garage, and I walked through the house and out the back to sit by the pool. I took off my shoes, pulled up the legs of my jeans and stuck my feet in the water. We'd been right there at the mall, and I still hadn't gotten a bathing suit.

The sound of water lapping woke me. I was lying curled in a chaise lounge, and a breeze was blowing around me, making me shiver. Clouds covered the sky, and the air was damp. It felt like rain.

I rolled off the lounge and got to my feet. I was stiff, and my neck was throbbing. I went in search of Hammie and found Moose in the kitchen eating chips. I dropped into the chair across from him, and he passed over the bowl.

"Want some? You slept through lunch."

"Where's Hammie?"

Moose couldn't keep the smile from his face.

"You have got to stop calling him that, it undermines his authority."

"You should stop encouraging me, then. You can't even keep a straight face when you're telling me I'm undermining him. Look, I'm supposed to be seeing a physical therapist. Hammie needs to take me to the doctor or something. I can't even turn my neck."

Moose pushed back his chair and walked to a console on the wall by the door. He pushed a button and spoke.

"Richard, we need you in the kitchen." Moose released the button.

"Right, I'll be down in a sec." Hammie's voice came from the wall.

"He was in the weight room." Moose plopped back down in his chair. "Working off his frustration."

Hambecker came into the room, wiping the sweat from his face with a hand towel. He had on sweats cut off at the knee and a sleeveless tee-shirt showing the muscles in his shoulders and chest. I pulled my eyes away.

"What's up?"

"The princess here needs to see a doctor." Moose nodded to me.

"I am not a princess. I injured my neck, and the ER doc told me to see a physical therapist, and then you abducted me. It hurts. I can't turn my head. See? I need PT."

"You can't turn your head. You can lead us on a wild goose chase through the biggest damn shopping mall in Sacramento County, but you can't turn your head. Right. Fine. I'll get you PT." He left the kitchen shaking his head.

"You're not an easy keeper, you know."

"I'm not an easy keeper?"

"Yeah, you know, you need a lot of upkeep." Moose was standing with his back to the sink, leaning on the counter.

"I own a farm, city boy. I know what an easy keeper is."

"I'm not a city boy, and don't get all worked up with me for telling you the truth."

"Listen, egghead. You wouldn't be an easy keeper either if you were in my shoes, so lighten up."

"Egghead? I thought an egghead was a smart guy. Oh, I get it; you're calling me a smart aleck. Yeah?"

"Yeah. Smart Aleck. That's it. You got me."

I grabbed a handful of chips and headed for the little library. I doubted anyone would bother me there.

I was well into a mystery when Moose came in with his hands full.

"Here," he said, "a hot pack for your neck. Lean forward."

I sat up and leaned forward so he could drape a warm towel around my neck.

"Be careful. They stay hot, and you probably need to keep the towel between the pack and your skin so you don't get burned."

"Thanks, Moose. That feels great."

He pulled a bottle from his back pocket.

"Ibuprofen," he said. "It'll help keep the inflammation down. Richard will get you a physical therapist, but it might take a day or two." He smiled at me. "I'm sorry I said you weren't an easy keeper."

He left. I felt the heat sink into the muscles in my neck and relaxed into it. He was a decent guy.

A day or two? How long did they plan on keeping me here? If I identified the two criminals, wouldn't that be the end of it? I started to think about Fogel. Was he looking for me? How was the senator going to explain my presence in his house? Was Fogel in on the whole thing?

The possibilities made my head hurt. I missed Meg and my dogs and Beau. An image of Beau laid up with a broken leg worrying but not being able to do anything ran through my mind. I wondered if he had Beans with him or if the Chihuahua was still at home with my dogs. I didn't think Tank would eat him, but I wasn't positive, and it made me nervous to think of it.

I looked out the window, past the pool and the palms, out to the empty valley leading to the foothills. I'd never be able to escape that way. Agent Truefellow was watching the front of the house. The only thing for me to do was to tell the senator I'd identify his criminals.

I got up, feeling a tiny bit less sore, and searched the room for a phone. None. I went to the kitchen, now empty of Hambecker and Moose. No phone here either. I opened the broom closet, no phone in there, and moved on to the living room, then game room. The house was devoid of telephones.

The sight of the stairs made me pause, but stiff or not, the senator's office was the most likely place for a phone. Although I didn't remember one. I climbed the stairs and took a left at the second floor landing. I stepped into the office and closed the door behind me, searching the room with my eyes. No phone. Crap, the senator had obviously embraced the get-rid-of-the-landline craze that was sweeping the country, and here I was without my cell phone. Great.

I stomped back downstairs, out through the French doors and along the cement path to the rear of the property. There was a distinct change at the edge of the property. Ferns, palms and manicured lawn gave way to a fifteen foot swath of mowed meadow grass on the downhill slope, which turned into uncut meadow half way down the hill.

The mowed path would make it easy to walk along behind the houses, but I suspected that everyone here had security cameras of their own. The edge of the properties to the right curved away so I could only see the yards for a short distance. The outward curve of the subdivision left the back sides of the houses exposed.

I walked to the corner of the senator's yard and looked around the wall into the neighbors' property. It was another beautifully landscaped garden with a pool taking up most of the space. The wall extended to the edge of the house on both sides. If there was a gate, I couldn't see it.

A movement behind me caught my attention. I turned to see Hambecker standing just outside the French doors, watching me. I raised my hand in a finger wave. If I stepped off the property, he'd be after me in a shot, no doubt. I migrated back to the pool and sat in a chaise and closed my eyes. More power to him, if he wanted to bore himself watching me take a nap.

A breeze sprang up and ruffled my hair. It was like spring in Vermont. I heard the scraping noise of a chair being pulled up beside me; it creaked as it took Hammie's weight. I refused to open my eyes and look at him.

"I found you a physical therapist," he said. "She'll be here this afternoon."

"That was fast." I was impressed despite myself.

"I called in a favor. My past life occasionally comes in handy."

"I can see that."

"You'd see more if you'd open your eyes."

"Literally or figuratively?"

"Both." He sighed. "I was happier in the Navy. The objective was precise, the chain of command was clear. We knew what we were doing and why we were doing it. It's hard to be effective without a clear objective."

"I can see that." I wasn't ever sure of my objectives, and it didn't bother me much.

"You're probably going to hate me for saying this, but I enjoyed abducting you. Get in, grab the target, get out. Get clear of the plane. All action. No sitting around and waiting. To tell you the truth, I probably could have taken you off the plane through the airport. All I had to do was flash a phone number, and it would have all worked out fine. It was just way more fun to cause a scene and disappear. That's what I do best."

I laughed. I couldn't help it. Poor Hammie, all muscle and training, stuck sitting around Wallace's house waiting for him to slip up, the opposite situation than what he was trained for.

"I don't know what to say. I can't say I'm happy to be the victim of a snatch-and-grab. I'm supposed to be at home, thinking about Christmas presents and taking care of my animals. My boyfriend has a broken leg, most likely courtesy of Wallace, and that's my fault. He can't finish the job he was working on, and I'm pretty sure he's worried about what happened to me. He probably thinks I'm dead, and they just haven't found the body yet."

The breeze had turned into a wind and a spattering of rain hit us and made ripples in the pool.

"Come on. Your neck will get all cold and stiff again out here."

I followed him back into the house and through to the kitchen where Moose was pulling food out of the fridge.

"You're cooking?" I asked.

"One of us had to do it, and Hambecker's not my first choice for chef. He burns everything."

"I like things well cooked," said Hammie. "A little carbon doesn't bother me, although I have to say I like Moose's cooking better than mine."

"My cooking consists of pulling a yogurt out of the fridge," I said, "so anyone is better than me. What are you making?"

"Soup and sandwiches, if I can find what I need. If I can't, I'm sending Hambecker to the store." He poured some chips in a bowl, dumped salsa in another and put them in front of me. "Eat this while I make some guacamole."

I dipped a chip in salsa while Moose halved an avocado and spooned it out of its shell. He stirred in some mayo, a squirt of lemon juice and dumped in some of the salsa and mixed it up. He plopped that in front of me too.

"Hey," Hambecker said. "What about me? Why does she get all the food?"

"She's more appreciative, and you've got a longer reach."

Before long, Moose had homemade chicken noodle soup on the stove and was toasting rolls for his hot turkey-with-cheese sandwiches. The kitchen smelled wonderful, and I stopped eating guacamole so that I'd have room for lunch. Hammie pulled three beers out of the icebox and popped the caps off.

"Beer for lunch?" I asked taking a drink. "Aren't you two still on duty?"

"I'm not planning to drive anywhere today," Moose said. "The senator's not here, and you are, so I'm cool."

"I figure as long as you're drinking beer, too, I'm okay. I only need to be as sharp as you are fast. My guess is that you are a lightweight and that beer is going to relax you and make you sleepy. Am I right?"

"Probably," I said. "Beer and ibuprofen. A good start to an afternoon nap."

"Don't go to sleep until after the physical therapist comes. She's going to want to talk to you."

Luckily, it wasn't long before she came, lugging her portable table and a carrier full of gear. We had her set up in the little library so I could watch the wind and rain while she worked, but in actuality, the sound of rain put me to sleep.

A gentle hand on my shoulder woke me.

"Time for me to go."

I didn't open my eyes.

"Can't I have five more minutes?"

"I'm sorry, I squeezed you in as a favor to Richard, but I really have to go now."

I groaned and sat up, swaying on the massage table.

"Here, let me help you." The massage therapist supported my arm and led me to an armchair in front of the window.

"Sit here until you feel more awake."

I closed my eyes, and when I opened them, she was gone.

# Nine

When I came out of the shower the next morning, the senator's voice was audible in the hall. My stomach clenched as I wrapped myself in the towel and hurried into my room to get dressed. He sounded jovial; obviously San Francisco had been a success. I rubbed my hair with the towel, finger-combed it, and took a quick look in the mirror. Mascara would help. Too bad I didn't have any.

Frustrated that I wasn't looking my best, I made my way into the kitchen where Senator Wallace was holding court over Hambecker, Moose, Paris and an attractive young dark-haired woman I assumed was his daughter.

The girls were perched on kitchen stools, elbows resting on the island. Hammie was leaning against the wall, and Moose was at the stove cooking eggs and pancakes. I assumed that Wallace had a chef, but every time I'd been served a meal in this house, Moose had cooked it.

Wallace was leaning against the sink counter, forcing Moose to walk around to the prep sink in the island when he needed water. Moose spotted me and smiled.

"Tea?" He grabbed the kettle and was halfway around the island before I could respond. I didn't have the heart to tell him I wasn't in the mood for anything, so I just nodded.

"Bree, how lovely. Let me introduce you to my daughter, Wendy. Wendy, this is the guest I told you about, Bree MacGowan.

I reached out my hand to shake her hand. She looked confused for a moment and then took it with a firm grip. I appreciated a firm handshake, nothing worse than shaking a hand that felt like a dead fish. She reminded me of Snow White with her dark wavy hair and blue eyes. All she needed were puffed sleeves and a blue apron.

"Dada tells me that you are going to help catch the men who killed my stepmom. That's great."

Well, that explained why she looked nothing like Lily Wallace. Stepmother.

"Yeah, well I hope I'm able to help. I'm not sure I'll recognize anyone, but I'll try."

Wallace beamed at me. "That's my girl, I knew you'd come around to my way of thinking. Feed this girl some breakfast, Marshall. We've got a long morning ahead of us."

The thought of food nauseated me, and I shook my head at Moose. He looked at me with eyebrows raised and mimicked my head shake with a frown.

"No food?" he mouthed. "Really."

"No food," I mouthed back. I turned back to the group to find them all looking at us.

"I'm really not hungry," I said. "I didn't want to be rude and refuse your hospitality, but something I ate yesterday didn't agree with me."

Wallace started to protest.

"No, really, I'll eat later. I just need some time for my stomach to settle."

Wallace shrugged, but Wendy fixed her baby blues on me. I turned away, uncomfortable under her gaze.

A couple of dogs started barking, and Wendy trotted out of the room. The French doors slammed, and she returned a moment later with a couple of corgis following her. They stopped when they saw me, and the fur rose on the darker dog's back.

I kept my side to them, endeavoring to be a little less threatening, and crouched down. This was either a really stupid or really smart thing to do, depending on the dogs.

In this case the gamble paid off. The dogs wiggled their way over to me and sniffed the hand I dangled at my side. A minute later I was cross-legged on the floor, the puppies had flopped over onto their backs, and I was rubbing their tummies.

Wendy joined me for the tummy-fest on the floor. The dogs reminded me of home, and I had to blink back tears. Moose knocked a box of tissues off the counter so I could wipe my nose.

"What's her name?" I asked as one of the corgis wriggled and squirmed her way into my lap.

"That's Fiddle, this is Bow." She scratched Bow behind the ears, and the dog made little grunting noises like a pig.

"Fiddle? Your name is Fiddle?" I made a fuss over the dog, and she stood up, put her front paws on my chest, and reached up to lick my chin.

"Wendy," Wallace said. "I thought I told you those dogs could only come if they stayed outside or in your room. I especially don't want them in the kitchen. Take them away."

Wendy got up and called Fiddle to her. Both dogs followed her out of the room.

"Ms. MacGowan, come with me."

I followed Wallace out of the room and up the stairs. I sat in the chair opposite his and stared around, feigning interest in his office. Wallace pulled a file out of a drawer in his desk and slid it across to me.

"I want you to memorize these faces. Take them to your room. Let me know when you've got them down, and I'll take you into Sacramento."

"How am I going to explain why I didn't remember these guys earlier?"

"A lot can be explained by the shock of finding a body. You won't be the first person to remember something after the fact."

I took the photos down to my room and taped them on the wall. I didn't have any intention of memorizing their faces, but if I didn't look like I was making an effort, Wallace would get suspicious. I was giving myself twenty-four hours. Then Wallace would take me to Fogel, and I'd be quit of this place. I'd get to go home.

I propped myself on the bed, facing the pictures in case anyone came in, but planning to close my eyes and take a nap. There was a tap at the door and Wallace walked in.

"I forgot something." He handed me another picture. "Just in case you were thinking you could tell Fogel something different than what we agreed."

I glanced down at the photo. It was Beau. He was standing on the side of a country road with the aid of crutches. The Foresthill Bridge stretched across the American River Canyon behind him.

"Where is he now?" My voice caught in my throat.

"Resting comfortably in my family's cabin in the mountains. Too bad he can't ski at the moment. As it is, I think he's bored, so I sent some people up there to keep him company. Men to help him get around and a couple of pretty girls to amuse him."

"How long has he been there?"

"A day or two. He's staying until my name is cleared. If you need to go on the witness stand, he'll stay until after you testify, just to keep you safe from attacks of conscience."

Wallace left, and I laid my head back and closed my eyes. Sneaky bastard. What was I going to do now? Beau would tell me to do the right thing, but I couldn't risk Wallace throwing him over the bridge. His chances of survival were slim, even if he didn't have a bullet in his head. No wonder the senator was in such a good mood. He had an ace in the hole. I was screwed.

I looked at the pictures on the wall and wondered what the two men were really guilty of. Nothing, maybe. Oh, crap. I pulled the edge of the comforter up over me, rolled over and closed my eyes. Okay, God, if you've got a way to get me out of this mess, now would be a good time to let me know what it is.

Another tap came at the door.

"Go away." I muttered. "No one's home."

I heard the door open but didn't open my eyes.

"Bree?" Wendy's voice was tentative. "Do you want to come run the dogs with me?"

"Where are you taking them?" I sat up in bed. I needed to get out of this house.

"If we walk along the back of the houses, we'll come to a little dog park. There's a kid park there, too, but they set aside an area just for dogs to run and do their business. Fiddle and Bow love to go there."

Wendy loaned me a sweatshirt so I wouldn't get cold, and we started out along the back of the houses, walking along the path. Wendy let the dogs off their leashes as soon as we were out of sight of the house.

"I'm not strictly allowed to have them off leash until we reach the park, but I don't pay attention to that rule unless my dad is with me. They don't get enough exercise, and I don't want them to get pudgy."

The corgis sprinted back and forth, running ahead, then running back to us. I was happy to be in the open air with no one watching me. Wendy was with me of her own free will and didn't have the need to keep me in her sights. The air was cool, maybe fifty-five degrees, and I had only a sweatshirt to wear, but we moved quickly, and I warmed up.

It took maybe ten minutes to walk to the dog park. It was fenced along three sides to prevent dogs from taking off after jackrabbits, was my guess, and keep the poop confined to one area. There were trees planted along the fence between the dog park and the kid park. The corgis sniffed and ran from place to place while we stomped our feet and slapped our arms to keep from going numb.

I turned and scanned the backs of the houses. They all had walled yards, the same as the homes near the senator's. There was someone watching us from the house directly behind the dog park. It had floor-to-ceiling windows like the senator's, and a person lurked behind the curtained French doorway.

"Look," I said, "someone is watching us."

Wendy turned and took in the view.

"Must not have anything better to do than to watch the people in the dog park all day," she said.

"Maybe it's the poop police checking to make sure everyone picks up after their dogs."

"There's a great job, spying on the neighbors."

"I can think of about a million things I'd rather do than that. Heck, I'd rather pick up the dog poop than spy on the neighbors."

"I think I'd draw the line at that," she said. "Picking up my own dogs' poop is bad enough. I'm not volunteering to pick up other people's dog poop."

"Or is it other people's dogs' poop?"

Wendy laughed. "Yeah, other people's dogs' poop."

I watched the houses as we walked back. There seemed to be people in most of them, either half-hidden in the garden or peering out of a window. I got a shiver up my spine.

"Cold?" Wendy asked me.

"Yeah. Let's get inside."

Which was worse: the devil you knew or the devil you didn't?

The next morning I told Wallace I was ready to ID the men. He smiled and told me he'd arrange a meeting as soon as Fogel was free. I was sick with relief on one hand and anxiety on the other. What if I couldn't talk to an officer alone? What if everything went irretrievably wrong?

I grabbed a book from the library and hid in my room. Wendy brought me clean clothes, and I used up part of the morning getting showered. I was antsy. I wanted to be on the move, away from this house. Being patient was killing me.

Hammie knocked on the door in the afternoon and asked if I wanted to come watch the football game. I declined; I didn't want to have to be friendly to Wallace, even if his daughter was really very nice. I cracked the book but couldn't concentrate on the words, so I walked over to the window and looked out on the day. Stinking Madison. Why did she have to give me back to Hammie? It would have made life so much easier if she'd just kept me.

I finally gave up planning my escape as a bad job and went out to join the family around the big flat screen TV in the living room. Moose was putting out snacks when I walked in. He gave me a wink and a smile, and I found myself smiling back despite myself. He was like a big goofy dog; I couldn't help but like him.

I squeezed myself in between Wendy and Hammie on the big couch. Wallace was sitting on the love seat with Paris. They were ignoring the game, heads bent together, chatting. If I'd been Hammie, I would have been feeling pangs of jealousy, but he was focused on the game and didn't seem the least troubled by the tête-à-tête on the love seat.

I found I couldn't really focus on the game. Alabama was playing Florida, a mishmash of red and white guys running around on the field. It's not that I don't like football. I love to watch with a group of friends, but this felt awkward. I thought Hammie was the only one watching the game, and I wasn't really sure about him. It was entirely possible he was playing possum.

I got up and wandered into the kitchen. Moose was sitting on a stool, watching the game on a screen that was normally disguised as a painting.

"Hey," I said. "How come you aren't out there with the rest of the Wallace retinue?"

"I'm not really comfortable hanging out with the boss." He shrugged. "Want something to drink?"

"Sure. Is there any soda? No, sit. I can get it. I walked to the silver fridge, but Moose shook his head.

"That's the food fridge. The beverages are in a drawer under the counter, next to the ice machine."

The glasses were in a cupboard next to the sink. I filled one with ice and grabbed a soda out of the beverage drawer.

"Since when do they refrigerate drawers?" I asked. "This kitchen is wild."

"Where you been? The rich and famous have had cold drawers for years."

"Not hanging out with the rich and famous, obviously, but even the ritzy hotel I used to work for didn't have drink drawers. They put dorm fridges in the rooms."

I popped the top on my soda and poured it into the glass. It immediately foamed up, and I bent and sipped the foam off the top.

"I always pour too much in. You'd think I'd learn."

"It's habit. You do it the same way every time without thinking. You want to change it, you have to focus on it."

"Guess I can't be bothered to focus on a soda."

"You can try putting your finger in it when it foams. Someone told me that works."

"If I remember," I said. I picked up my soda. "I think I'll take this back to my room. I've got faces to memorize."

"I don't think you should be talking about that. Be careful."

"Wallace didn't tell me not to talk, so I assumed everyone in the house knew what was going on except Wendy. I have the feeling he didn't tell her the whole truth."

"Probably not."

"Who do you think did the actual killing?"

"I don't watch that show." He looked around and whispered in my ear. "You need to watch what you say. The walls may not have ears, but they definitely have bugs. Wallace doesn't leave anything to chance."

A puff of air escaped me. I wasn't going to be getting any information from Moose. I was pretty sure he was some kind of agent, too, but maybe not. Do agents pretend to be chefs? Probably, if it got them where they needed to be. The stool tipped and righted itself as I slid to the floor. My glass had started to sweat, and I grabbed a napkin to use as a coaster.

"Going back to your room? I'm thinking you spend too much time alone in there."

"Well, I can't very well study those pictures out here."

I glanced back into the kitchen from the hall. Moose was pulling Plexiglas parts out of a cabinet under the island.

"What's that?"

It's a fountain. I'm going to put melted chocolate in it. Serve pretzels and berries to dip in it. Fresh pineapple slices. Stuff like that."

"Where did you learn to cook?"

"Oh, you know. Took a crash course in chauffeuring and cooking from the Chauffeuring and Cooking Institute." He laughed.

He got the fountain assembled, and I migrated back into the kitchen, watching. He stuck chocolate into the microwave to melt and started pulling trays of fruit out of the big fridge.

"Did you prepare all that stuff?" I asked.

"Nah." Moose smiled. "Bought it like this from the grocery store. No shortage of money in this house, so I take the easy way." He pulled packages of shortbread cookies and pretzels out of the pantry and added sprinkles and doodads. Then he carried the fountain out of the kitchen, presumably to put it on the dining room table. I looked at the chocolate melting in the microwave and was struck by a thought. I set my soda on the counter and jogged down the hall to the bathroom.

The shelves in the medicine cabinet were disappointing. Tums, Tylenol and toothpaste. Nothing useful. I ran up the stairs to the master bedroom, crossing my fingers that Wallace wouldn't catch me there. I hit the jackpot. Chocolate laxative, ipecac and diet pills. Stuffing the pockets of my jeans with likely items, I looked further. Two bottles of Valium. Bingo! Prescription drugs make me nervous, and I toyed with leaving them. I slipped them in my pocket anyway, just in case.

Downstairs, I unloaded my pockets and shoved everything under my pillow. I wandered back into the kitchen and picked up my soda. Moose was stirring the melted chocolate.

"Not quite done," he said and put the bowl back in the microwave.

"Moose? Is there a computer where I can do some shopping? I'd like some stuff, and I thought I could put some stuff in a cart, and the senator could pay for it and have it shipped. Do you think that would be all right?"

"Sure. See this cabinet over here?" He opened what looked like a pantry. Inside was a laptop computer, a printer on the shelf above and a scanner beside it. Three digital cameras were plugged into their docks, all charged up and waiting for someone to come along and use them.

"Thanks." I sat down and pulled up the website for Old Navy. I signed in and pulled up an old wish list. There was enough stuff in the list to cover any need I might have except underwear and bras, so I added the first matching cotton bras and panties that came up on the search and saved the entire wish list to my cart. I looked around. Moose was fussing with burgers now, slicing tomatoes and flipping patties.

Leaving the cart showing to the side, I opened a new page and pulled up a search engine. Keeping an eye on Moose I searched the effects of the drugs I'd pilfered from the medicine chest. Then on a whim I searched the combination of laxatives and ipecac. Three minutes of reading convinced me that the ipecac was going back in the cupboard. I wasn't interested in killing anybody. The laxatives and diet pills, however, had definite possibilities.

I cleared the browser history, although it was doubtful anyone would be looking for it until after I'd already done the damage. I left the shopping cart up on the screen. If things didn't go the way I wanted, at least I'd have new underwear.

Moose took a tray of fruit into the dining room, and I helped myself to an extra large mug from the cabinet, taking it down the hall and into my room. I locked myself in my bathroom and unwrapped all the laxatives, shoving them into the cup.

Trying to look as if nothing's up when you're carrying around a mug full of stool softener isn't easy. I felt a complete fool, and my heart was banging away, making me feel flustered. I smiled at Moose as he passed me with a bowl of chips and hurried over to the microwave. I set the timer and nuked the laxative. You can learn some very interesting things on the web.

Moose came back in the kitchen as I was pulling the mug from the microwave. I smiled at him, trying to look innocent and feeling like a complete failure.

"Make yourself some hot chocolate?" he asked.

"I hope that's okay."

"Sure. Make yourself at home." He grabbed a beer and headed for the living room.

I made my way into the dining room, admiring the beautiful fountain and fruits. I snagged a piece of pineapple and bit into it, wiping the juice from my face. I poured the melted laxative into the fountain, snagged a strawberry and took the mug into the kitchen. I rinsed it out and dried it. I wandered back down the hall into my bathroom, trying to look inconspicuous and probably failing horribly. Luckily no one came into the hall to see me. After locking the door, I grabbed the diet pills and pried open the capsules. I dumped the powder into my mug and snuck back into the dining room.

I mixed the powder into the spicy guacamole and the cocktail sauce for the shrimp, using the serving spoons to make sure there weren't any traces. The next part was going to be more difficult, the Valium needed to be crushed. Back in the bathroom, I put the pills on the marble counter and looked around for something heavy and hard to smash them with. One blow with the ceramic soap dispenser cured me of that idea. It sounded like I was trying to demolish the bathroom. I put the pills on the tile floor, pulled off my sneakers and slid on the blue heels. I stepped on the pills one at a time, crushing them under my heel. A piece of paper from the little desk worked as a scooper, and I poured the powder back into the prescription bottle, trying not to feel too guilty about the dirt from the floor and shoe.

I rejoined the family and stood in the archway to the living room. Wallace was drinking scotch. I leaned against the door jam waiting. It wasn't long before he was waving his empty glass in the air.

"Mr. Moore! Refill!"

"I've got it," I said, reaching over the back of the couch and snagging his glass from his hand. I took it over to the bar. I checked to make sure that everyone still had their backs to me and pulled the prescription bottle out of my pocket. My hands were trembling, and I had trouble getting the lid off. I shook some of the crushed Valium into the glass. *God, please keep me from killing anyone.* I added Scotch and stirred with my finger.

A while later I realized that I was going to have to do more than knock the senator out. The girls weren't eating the drug-laced food. Wendy had a couple of pieces of fruit with a miniscule amount of chocolate, but not enough to really incapacitate her. Paris wasn't eating at all. I shook Valium into the blender with the margaritas, ignoring the panic building in my belly.

Eventually the drugs began to take effect. The girls were asleep in front of the TV. Moose had disappeared into the bathroom off the kitchen, Hammie was upstairs, and the senator was incoherent.

"What's wrong with me?" he asked for the tenth time as I tried to get him down the hall to the limo.

"Everybody's sick," I lied. "I need to get you to the hospital. I'm the only one left who's well enough to drive."

"But why are we sick?" He put the emphasis on why, like a child.

"Ate something bad, I guess. Maybe it was the shrimp cocktail, I didn't have any of that."

"Maybe the shrimp." He sounded as if he was drifting off again, and I could feel him growing heavier. "Senator Wallace." I shoved him upright. "You have to stay awake until you are in the car." I pushed him along the hall. If he passed out, I'd never get him down the steps in the garage or into the limo for that matter.

"Car," he said.

"Yeah, car. Come on."

I opened the door to the garage with my left hand while steadying him with my right. I edged out the door and stepped down the stars backward. Luckily there were only three of them, and he didn't fall flat on his face. He was leaning on me heavily and dragging his feet. I leaned him against the side of the first limo and opened the door. His knees gave way, and he slid down the side of the car and sat on the floor of the garage.

I grabbed an arm and tugged.

"Senator! Get in the car. We have to get you to the hospital."

"I'm coming." His words slurred and his head dropped.

"Shit!" I left him sitting there and ran back into the house. The kitchen was a disaster of dishes. I grabbed a half-empty beer mug off the island and topped it off with water. I took it back into the garage and threw it in the senator's face.

He spluttered and coughed.

"In the car, Senator Wallace. Get in the car."

He gave up trying to stand and crawled to the door of the car, where he rested his forehead on the edge of the seat.

"In you go." I prodded him with my foot, and he crawled into the back and collapsed on the back seat. "Stay there. I'll be right back."

At the driver's door I scanned the controls until I found the one I thought locked the back doors from the inside. I found Moose in the bathroom sitting on the edge of the tub, his head between his knees.

"Moose."

Moose slowly raised his head and looked at me.

"I need the keys to the limo."

"In the laundry room." He swallowed hard. "Was it the chocolate or the beer?" he asked.

"Both." I felt a small twinge of guilt. I'd seen him sample both.

"Oh, God. I'll never eat chocolate again." He dropped his head to his knees and then sat up and lunged for the toilet.

I backed out of the bathroom. A cell was ringing. I heard Hammie answer as I walked past the living room. I slowed to listen.

"Yeah? You're in the limo? Can you tell where you are?" He paused, and I could hear him taking deep breaths. His stomach was probably cramping, but he hadn't had much of the poison margaritas. I heard him take a drink of something. Most of the drinks in the living room were now laced with Valium. I almost felt bad for him.

"You're in the garage? The garage here at the house? The car is locked. Well, sit tight, someone will come out to get you in a bit." I moved on. I needed to be out of there before he pulled himself together.

"No, she can't take you anywhere, she doesn't know where the keys are kept."

I left him to reason with Wallace and trotted down to the laundry room and stopped dead. Where in the laundry room? I pulled out drawers and rummaged through the cupboards in a panic. Nothing. I stopped and looked around, scanning the walls. There was a cabinet-sized mirror set into the wall next to the door. I tried pulling it open, but I couldn't get my fingers around the edges of the frame. I put my palm on it and pushed. It popped out, revealing a wall full of keys.

Not knowing which were the keys to the limo Wallace was in, I pulled a set of every key chain with a push button fob and headed out to the garage. Once in the driver's seat of the limo, I almost chickened out. There were a lot of buttons and doodads that were a mystery. But I found the place to stick the key, and the shifter was right where it should be. To hell with it, the rest of that stuff could just take care of itself.

I pressed the remote for the garage door and started the car. So far, so good. I put it in gear and eased out through the door and down the drive. Except for being really long, it handled pretty much like any other boat. I turned right onto the street and heard something scrape the side of the car. The mailbox toppled. Great. By the time this was over, I'd be replacing half a mil's worth of stuff.

The gate to the complex went up as we approached. I drove through without looking at the guardhouse. I braced myself for the gate to come crashing down on us, but we got through free and clear. Hammie must not realize the seagull had left the building.

I maneuvered the big car out onto the freeway and headed north. If Wallace had a cabin, I was betting it was not far from Foresthill—more specifically, the Foresthill Bridge. The privacy window was up between the front and back seats. I pushed a likely looking button, and the sunroof rolled back. Okay, don't need that at the moment. Closed the sunroof and tried again.

This time the privacy window slid down. I was worried about Wallace coming over the seat and trying to throttle me, so I stopped it at about five inches. Enough so he could hear me, not so much that he could get through the window and kill me.

"Senator Wallace. Wake up."

He didn't move.

"Hey. Wake up!"

Still nothing. I turned on the radio full blast.

"What!" Senator Wallace sat up. "Turn it off! Turn it off!"

I turned the radio off.

"Are you trying to make me deaf?"

"I need to know where your cabin is."

"Like I would tell you where my cabin is. You must think I'm stupid."

Yep, I did think he was stupid, but I wasn't telling him that.

"I put something stronger in Wendy's drink. It's potentially lethal but slow acting. You take me to the cabin, and I'll call and tell Hambecker to take her to the hospital. You don't take me, and there's a chance that she dies. It's up to you." I was feeling ruthless and desperate.

"No. I won't be blackmailed." He was shaking his head, but his eyes were closed.

"What will your constituency think of you when they find out you could have saved your daughter but didn't? Don't think you'll be in office too long, do you? Could you recover from that? Not without seeming like a callous bastard." I sounded pathetic even to myself.

"Fuck you. All you had to do was implicate two slimy cheese balls, and your life would have gone back to normal. They're crooks, rapists, thieves, fucking scum. And you're too high and mighty to finger innocent men. Let me tell you, Sweetheart, those guys are nowhere near innocent."

"Don't care what they are. I. Don't. Lie. Period." I crossed my fingers as I said it, trying not to think when the last lie was. Almost everything I'd said since we'd been in the car, but not the essentials, the essentials were true. At least that way I could justify myself.

We were coming into downtown Sacramento. I put on the signal and pulled onto the off ramp.

"Where are you going?" Wallace asked.

"Jail. No point in driving all over the foothills looking for a cabin in the middle of nowhere. I'll take you to the police and let them deal with you." I followed the signs toward the courthouse and Police Department.

"All right," he said, "all right, I'll take you. Just get back on the freeway and go east."

We drove up Interstate 80 for an hour. We passed Auburn and the Foresthill exit. I was in familiar territory now. I'd spent a month driving around this area scoping out photo opportunities. It was another forty-five minutes before Wallace told me to get off the freeway, and we followed winding back roads into the woods. The condition of the roads got steadily worse until we were bouncing along a barely paved road in the pines.

We came to a place where the road petered out, narrowing down to a track that the limo was too wide to navigate. It didn't feel right to me. I stopped the car and turned to look at Wallace.

"What now? The car won't make it down this track."

"We have to walk in from here. It's not too far, a quarter mile or so. Let me out of the back, and I'll show you the way."

Somehow I didn't see the Senator as the type of guy who would want to walk into his ski cabin. If it was a hunting cabin, maybe, but if I'd heard Fogel correctly, this was their base for hitting the slopes. They'd have all kinds of gear to carry besides suitcases, food and beer.

"No, I think I'll leave you here. I don't want to have to watch you while I'm helping Beau get back to the car." I rolled up the privacy window and looked at him in the mirror. His face was red with fury. He began pounding the window. He turned and kicked at the door, but this car was built to keep people in. He was trapped.

I wasn't about to crack open the privacy window, so I found the button for the intercom and pressed it on.

"I take it this isn't where your cabin is located? I'm going to back out of here. If you don't take me straight to Beau, I'll take you straight to Fogel. I take that back. First I'll call the *Sacramento Bee* and tell them my story, and then I'll take you to Fogel. You may be able to get him to hush things up, but you'll have a hard time hushing up every paper in the state."

The cabin, when we reached it, was about what I'd expected, a scaled-down ski lodge built above a huge two-bay garage. A group of people in jackets and beanies were sitting on the deck, enjoying the late afternoon sun. Beau wasn't among them.

I cracked the window and called out.

"Hey! Can one of you come to the railing, please?"

A rough-looking man of about forty walked over. He managed to look menacing just standing there. I took a look at his face and realized it was the city boy I'd seen from the tree. He was the suit from the river.

"What do you want?" he asked.

"I've got your boss in the back of the car. He needs you to bring Beau down."

"I'm not bringing anybody down until I talk to the senator."

I cracked the back window, just enough so he could see the senator's face, and spoke into the intercom.

"Tell him to bring Beau down to the car."

"Bring our guest out to the car," Wallace said, "and make it quick. I'm in a hurry."

"Are you sure, Senator Wallace? This wasn't in the instructions."

"Plans change, bring him out."

I sat on pins and needles as the minutes ticked by. The longer it took, the more antsy I got. Finally I pushed the intercom button.

"Where were your guys keeping him? You got a dungeon under this place?" If they had damaged a hair on Beau's head I was going to be really upset.

"I have no idea what's taking him so long. Not my idea, I assure you."

We sat a minute more before the door opened onto the deck, and Beau walked out followed by the senator's henchman. My heart leapt. Beau was on crutches, but otherwise he looked normal, at least at first glance. When my eyes lit on his face, I knew something was wrong. His mouth was tight and jaw clenched. That was when I saw the gun.

"Good man, Guy." I could hear the smile in Wallace's voice.

"Bastard. Shit." I locked the doors, and my mind went into overdrive trying to figure out how I was going to get Beau away from Guy. I started the car and revved the engine and put it in gear. I could miss Beau and hit Guy, couldn't I? Guy put the gun to Beau's head, and my stomach clenched.

For one crazy moment I imagined myself throwing the car into gear and taking the bastard out, but it was fleeting. I couldn't risk Beau. On a whim I reached over and opened the glove compartment, but unless I could knock Guy on the head with the owner's manual, I was out of luck.

Beau was yelling at me to drive away, but what was the point? If I drove Wallace away, chances were they'd hurt Beau. He didn't deserve that. Crap, crap, crap. I could drive Wallace to Fogel. There was a chance that Beau would be okay.

"You put that limo in gear, I shoot the guy." Guy stuck the barrel of the gun against Beau's cheek. "It's time for you to let Senator Wallace out of there."

It was probably my imagination, but I'd swear I saw his trigger finger tighten. I popped the locks on the rear of the car. Wallace shot out before I could change my mind.

"Give me the gun." He motioned for Guy to hand him the firearm. Guy looked confused, but when the senator held out his hand, he gave him the gun. Beau jerked out of Guy's grasp the moment Wallace took possession. The look Wallace gave me was of pure hatred. He leveled the gun at me and pulled the trigger.

# Ten

I had no idea what happened when bulletproof glass took a hit. I threw myself down on the seat, covering my head with my arms. I expected glass to go flying. There was a huge crack, but nothing happened. I rolled over and looked up at the window. The bullet had left a spider web of cracks.

I sat up just in time to see Wallace throw the handgun on the ground and kick it into the trees.

"Shit! Shit!" He was hopping around holding the foot that kicked the gun. He was wearing leather house slippers, and he had kicked the gun hard. I figured he'd broken a toe at the very least. I looked over to where Guy was standing. He was staring at Wallace with his mouth open. You'd think he had never seen a senator kick a gun and hurt his toe.

Beau was taking advantage of Guy's distraction, moving away as stealthily as he could on crutches. I waited until there was a good car's width between Beau and Guy. I started the limo, threw it into gear, and skidded between the men. I held my breath as I popped the locks open so Beau could dive in, then took off backward before he even had his crutches in the car.

Guy lunged for my door and got it open before I could flip the locks shut. We were zooming backward, Guy hanging on to the door for dear life as Beau tried to get his crutches in the car and the door shut. I screamed along in reverse as far as I dared and slammed on the brakes. Guy lost his hold, and both doors slammed shut.

I jammed the gearshift into drive and went roaring down the road in the direction we'd come in from.

"You kidnapped that old coot?" Beau asked. I nodded my head, and he laughed. "My God, you've got balls. Who was he?"

"Senator Wallace. He was using you to blackmail me. I was supposed to tell Fogel I saw these two guys up at the river when his wife died. He was going to hold you until I did what he said. He actually kidnapped me before I kidnapped him, so I think we're even."

"What are we doing now? Heading home?"

"If I can find my way back to the freeway, I'm taking us to Fogel. I need to tell him what's going on."

"Did they treat you all right?" I looked over at him. He looked good. If it wasn't for the broken leg, I'd say he was in fine fighting form.

"I didn't even know I was kidnapped until you arrived. Some guy called me and said a senator wanted me to look at his property and give an estimate for some masonry work. I said I couldn't make it for a while, and they offered me a lot of money just to look and do the design. So I thought what the hell and came. Every day there's been something new for me to look at, design, what have you. I was downstairs figuring a dry stone wall when Guy came down and asked me to come upstairs. We were out the door before I realized he had a gun and you were in the car. The rest you know."

I focused my attention on the road. The limo wasn't the easiest thing to drive, especially on these dinky winding roads. If somebody was bombing up the hill and didn't see me around one of the corners … I didn't want to think about it.

"Get your seatbelt on, would you? This road worries me."

"Want me to drive? Couldn't be worse than driving a fire truck."

"Are you kidding? I'm not letting you drive with a broken leg."

I negotiated a hairpin turn, pleased that the back end hadn't ended up in the ditch, and heard Beau suck in his breath.

"What?" I said, but I saw. Wallace's other limo was blocking the road ahead of us.

I shoved the brake to the floor and the back end broke loose, sending us skidding sideways toward the other limo. The rear tires slid off the road into the ditch, and the undercarriage scraped along the rocky surface. My jaw ached with the noise, and the hair on the back of my neck stood up. I glanced over at Beau. His hands were over his ears.

The length of the car slammed full into the other limo, bouncing my head off the window. Tears and flashes of light blocked my vision, but I heard yells from the other limo.

"Those bastards were expecting you to crash into them. Lock the doors."

But I still couldn't see. My fingers fumbled along the armrest feeling for the controls. Beau lurched across me and slammed the master lock. The doors clicked front and rear. They clicked unlocked and Beau hit the button again. The doors locked and unlocked. My vision cleared, and I saw Hammie climbing around the front of his limo, a black key-fob in his hand. Either both cars worked on the same frequency, or he had the spare.

There was movement in the rearview mirror. Moose was climbing around the back of the limo. Wendy and Paris were standing a ways down the road, holding Fiddle and Bow. The dogs were barking, adding to the general hullaballoo.

The locks clicked twice again. I pushed my hand under Beau's.

"I've got it," I said to Beau. "You think of a way to get us out of this."

"You want me to think of a way out of this? Sweetheart, I think we're screwed. Those guys have guns. What do we have? Nothing, as far as I can tell."

"The car is bulletproof. We've got that. And maybe I can figure out how to jam the locks so they can't keep opening them."

I tried starting the car. The engine caught, and I put it in gear. This caught Hammie off guard, and he forgot to unlock the door. Unfortunately, I was anticipating him unlocking so I hit the button for him. My fingers scrambled at the button again and I managed to lock it again before Moose opened the back door. Hammie came and stood at my door.

"Bree! Crack your window so I can talk to you." He was yelling but I could barely hear him. "I promise I won't try anything while we're talking. Okay? Truce."

Beau put his hand on my arm.

"MacGowan, keep your finger on the lock, and watch out. I'll keep an eye on his buddy. We'll roll down my window so he can't put the barrel of the gun through the crack."

Beau rolled his window down a couple of inches.

"I can hear you now," I said. "Talk."

"Are either of you hurt?" he asked.

This threw me off. He kept making me think that he cared, the bastard. It was so annoying. I looked at Beau.

"You hurt?" I asked.

He shook his head.

"We're fine, what do you want?"

"You don't look fine. You've got a bruise on your face. You need to make sure that you didn't fracture your skull." He looked over at Moose, who was standing at the rear door. I searched the dash for the privacy window controller.

"Help me figure out how to roll up the privacy window," I hissed at Beau. "Then it won't matter if they get in the back."

"I told you this wasn't a good idea." Hammie was talking to Moose. "She's hurt."

I saw Moose shrug in the wing mirror. "You didn't come up with anything better," he said.

Hammie turned his attention back to me. "Listen. You're going to have to come out of there sooner or later. You don't have any food or water. You can't watch over the locks indefinitely. Why don't you let me take you to the hospital?"

"Sooner or later," I said, "someone is going to come down the road. They'll call a tow truck and the cops, and I'll be free of you. I can watch the locks for as long as that takes." Stupid! I slapped my palm to my forehead and immediately regretted it as pain shot through my cheek. I turned to Beau. "Can you look around in the center console? I'm pretty sure there's a phone in here or one of those buttons that calls emergency services. We can get the cops to come to us."

Beau turned his attention to the electronic doodads in the control panels. I heard the locks click open and before I could react the back door was open, and Moose had a gun to my head.

"Moose! You've got a gun to my head. What are you thinking? Someone could get killed." I turned and looked into his eyes. "I don't believe this. You're going to kill me because I tried to escape? Un-effing-believable. I'm ashamed of you."

"You kidnapped my boss. What did you expect me to do?"

"Your boss is a filthy murderer. He killed his wife for money and power. What does that make you?"

The gun wavered from my head. Moose looked down. "Wallace wants you back, so I have to bring you back. It's as simple as that."

"What do you mean, it's as simple as that?" Beau was hopping mad. "You'd kill an innocent woman because your boss asked you to? On orders? You're just a couple of thugs dressed up with nice girls and dogs." Beau spat on the floor at his feet. "You going to kill us in front of them?" He motioned to Wendy and Paris who were still standing a ways up the road, horrified. "I doubt it." Beau knocked the gun away from my head, and Moose pointed it at him.

"Will you two stop it?" I unlocked the car and got out. Moose looked from me to Beau, unsure of who to follow, but Hammie stepped up and took me by the arm. He beckoned the girls to follow us.

"We're going up to the cabin."

Hambecker and I took the lead with Moose trailing Beau and the girls, who were bringing up the rear. Hambecker had a lock grip on my arm, and my hand was starting to feel numb, but I'd be damned if I'd ask him to loosen it. I'd show him I was tougher than I looked.

We hadn't walked more than a quarter of a mile when a white jeep came bombing down the road. A spark of hope rose in my chest, then fell again. It was Wallace's goon from the cabin. He made a three-point turn and stopped. Hambecker—I refused to think of him as Hammie ever again—shoved Beau and me into the middle of the back seat, while he and Moose perched on the outside, hanging onto the doorframe. Paris and Wendy squeezed into the front passenger seat, the dogs tucked in their laps. I took a last look at the limos wedged sideways in the road and said a small prayer that no innocent people would get hurt.

Beau's eyes were shut on the trip back up the hill. I wanted to ask him if his leg was hurting, but I knew he wouldn't admit to it in front of Moose and Hambecker. I really needed to remember Moose's real name. He'd shown his true colors, and in my estimation he'd lost all right to a nickname. These two were as slimy as Wallace.

There was no one in sight as we pulled up in front of the mini ski lodge. The girls jumped out, and the dogs hopped out of their arms and ran tree to tree, sniffing. Nothing like girls with dogs to make everything seem normal. I looked away. Beau's crutches had been left behind. I couldn't remember if he'd had them when he had gotten out of the limo, but regardless, they were gone. He leaned on my shoulder as we mounted the steps to the deck and in through the door that led to the living room.

We were led through a hall and down a flight of stairs into a huge stone room.

It was furnished like a studio apartment. There were a couple of couches arranged to take advantage of the view of the hillside. A small kitchen area was built into one side of the room, and a canopy bed took up a great deal of space toward the back, behind where the staircase came down. Across from the kitchen a drafting table held designs and blueprints. This must be where Beau had been working.

I walked over to the drawing table and flipped through the pictures. Beau had transformed the room we were standing in. The windows encompassed the entire wall. The stone wall across from the kitchen would be broken up by a gigantic fireplace and hearth. A knee wall would separate the sleeping area from the rest of the room, and I could see from the floor plan that there was a bathroom hiding under the stairs.

"Is this bathroom part of the original building?" I asked.

"What? Oh, yeah. Feel free, if you need to use it, but remember, it's a guy bathroom, okay. I don't want to hear about how disgusting it is."

I went into the room with trepidation, but it turned out not to be so bad. The shower wasn't black with dirt, and the toilet looked as though someone was cleaning it regularly. The sink and mirror had toothpaste splatters, and there wasn't a towel for hand drying. I dried my hands on Beau's shower towel and went to join him on the couch.

He had propped up his casted leg on the cushions and had his head resting on the arm of the couch. I dropped onto the other couch and relaxed into the pillows.

"Nice space," I said. The places I'd been confined flitted through my brain. Tom's office, a room at the posh hotel where I used to work. The trunk of a car. This was by far the most comfortable. That didn't make it any less menacing.

"I used to like this room," Beau said, "when I didn't know it was a cell. Let's go out the window and steal the Jeep."

"We should wait until they've had time to clear the limos out of the road, or we'll be trapped." I looked around for a clock. "I figure another hour should do it."

"Seems reasonable. I'm going to take my stuff."

Beau hobbled around the room, picking up his clothes and packing them into his suitcase. He limped and grimaced when he put weight on the casted leg, but he didn't complain. He paused at the drafting table and rolled up the drawings. These he shoved in the top of his backpack.

Beau headed back toward the bathroom, and I went to stand by the windows. The view of the mountains was spectacular, but what I wanted to see was if there was a way around the house. There was enough flat ground that we could get out the window, but I had no idea what we'd find when we rounded the corner. I hoped Beau would be able to manage with his luggage and cast.

Beau had his suitcase open on the bed when the upper door opened. Moose stood on the upper landing and looked around. He couldn't see Beau or his suitcase, thank goodness.

"Wallace wants to see you."

"Both of us or just me?"

"Just you."

I glanced at Beau and hoped he could read my mind. He could get help while Wallace was distracted.

I climbed the stairs and followed Moose down the hall into the main living area. It was another huge room with a freestanding fireplace right in the middle of the room. A copper hood and chimney hung from the ceiling, sucking up the smoke from the fire. I could feel the heat five feet away.

Wallace was sitting on one of the couches with a view of the deck and the hills beyond. I veered away from the fireplace and sat on the couch opposite him.

"You wanted to see me?"

"I've been going about this thing the wrong way, appealing to your sense of civic duty. Obviously, you don't care who they let loose in California. Can't blame you. I'd feel the same way if we were talking about Vermont."

"You have no idea," I started, but the senator held up his hand to silence me.

"It doesn't matter," he said. "I realized I need to make this a life-altering experience for you. You need an incentive. Put simply, if you ID those two men, I'll see to it you never have to work again. You can work if you want to, of course, but you'll be set financially. You'll get to choose." Wallace smiled at me. "But if you don't do as I ask, I'll see that you never work again."

"Are you out of …"

"Oh, I know," he interrupted me again. "You can always find someone to hire you as a waitress or a maid, a babysitter or a stable hand. But you'll never have a real job again, a meaningful job. Your newly fledged career as a reporter will certainly be over, and you won't be going back to work at that swank hotel they've got hidden out in the sticks. A maid with a criminal record wouldn't go over well there, I'm sure."

I closed my mouth. Wallace thought I could be bought or blackmailed or both, but I could turn this to my advantage. I just needed time to figure out how. I needed to talk to Beau, if he wasn't already gone.

"I want to …"

"Don't make a hasty …" he started.

I lost my temper. Damn it, there's only so much interruption a girl can take.

"Will you stop interrupting me? You win. I'll think it over, but I want to talk to Beau, as well. I'll come up when I've made up my mind." I thought briefly about telling him I'd knock on the upper door but decided against it. I needed to keep the illusion of control, if only for my own sanity.

I rose and walked out of the room. Wallace hadn't spoken since I'd yelled at him. Was this good or bad? I didn't know, so I hotfooted it out of the room as fast as I could without looking like I was beating a hasty retreat. Which, of course, I was.

Beau was at the window with his suitcase and backpack when I came back in the room. His frown disappeared when he saw it was me.

"Thank God," he said. "I was wondering if I needed to break in, guns blazing, and rescue you."

"Do you have a gun?"

"No, no gun, just a figure of speech."

"Oh." I thought a moment about the merit of guns. "Too bad. Listen, Wallace wants to buy me off. He said he'd set me up for life if I ID'd those two guys. I'm thinking we can use this to escape. I'll insist that I see Sheriff Fogel, and then I'll tell him Wallace is blackmailing me. We'll be free. Or something like that."

"I still think we should escape. That way we don't have to worry about either of us being held as hostage while he gets what he wants. Because whatever he says about money, he'll use our relationship to elicit cooperation. He's already proven that."

"I'm game. Do we go now?"

"I think we'd better wait until nightfall. Too many people checking out the view during the day, and we can't afford to be spotted." He stashed his luggage behind the coffee table where it couldn't be seen from the stairs and sat down on the couch. "Come sit with me. I want to hear what happened. I didn't even know you were back in California."

"You didn't know I was gone? How long have you been here?"

"Look at the dates on my plans. A week at the very least, merrily designing projects to do when my leg heals."

"You almost get killed falling off sabotaged scaffolding, and you come back here anyway? Didn't it occur to you that it could be a trap?"

"I recognized Wallace's name and figured a senator would be safe enough. If I disappeared, he'd know to go looking. It didn't occur to me that he was in on the murder."

"Lily Wallace. She was the money behind the man. Wallace doesn't have any of his own. If she left he'd be ruined. He murdered her or had her murdered, if he didn't actually pull the trigger."

"What does he want with you?"

"He says he'll make me independently wealthy if I claim that these two criminals did it. Why he thinks it will work, I don't know. I already told Fogel I didn't see anything."

"People forget things when they are in moments of high stress. Fogel would probably believe you if you told him you remembered seeing someone. It would take the heat off Wallace and give him room to breathe. What did you tell him?"

"I take exception to being told to lie and perjure myself. I was thinking of telling Senator Wallace that I'd talk to Fogel and then somehow slip a note to Fogel so he'd know the truth. But I do think getting away would be better. Get away, find Fogel and tell him that Wallace has been holding me captive. That would be the safer thing to do." And more satisfying.

"You never want to do anything the easy way, do you?"

"Easy shmeasy. I don't want the bad guy to get to do things his way. Anyway, I'm sure he'd find a way to foul up my plan, so we're getting out of here."

I got up and examined the possibilities for escape. The windows didn't open, of course. I was pretty sure if we broke one, an alarm would sound. I paced up and down thinking of options. There was nothing for it. We were going to have to go through the main house. Crap.

A quiet tap at the door interrupted my planning. Beau, who had been lounging on the couch watching me, sat up, concern on his face. The lock turned, and Wendy stepped through the door and closed it behind her. She ran lightly down the stairs to me.

"Paris and I have been planning," she said quietly, "we're going to get you out of here. I don't know what my dad's up to, but I'm sure it's wrong. My mom told me he didn't know right from wrong. That's why she divorced him."

"So why do you hang out with him?" I asked.

"I don't. I was completely surprised when he showed up at school. He doesn't normally have much to do with me, only when he wants something from me." The features of her face darkened momentarily, then she smiled. "Come on, I have something to show you."

Wendy led us past the bed and the bathroom to a bookcase against the wall. She dropped a couple of books on the floor and pulled a key out of her pocket. I moved up behind her so I could see there was a keyhole in the back of the bookcase. She inserted the key and yanked on what I had assumed was a decorative knob for hanging towels on the wall between the bathroom door and the shelves. The whole wall, books and all, swung forward, revealing a doorway into a typical basement storage area.

Beau looked at me and shrugged. We followed her past sleds, skis and snowboards. There were a couple of ski machines at the back near a set of garage doors and a light went on in my head. Under the deck at the front of the house were a couple of garage doors. I hadn't given a thought to them, but of course the main rooms of the house were upstairs. Beau's room was on the same level as the garage basement. Street level.

"We need to wait until they tow the limos up here." Wendy went to a small window in the garage door. "Paris is going to make sure the Jeep isn't blocked. We're bored and fed up with the thugs Dad's got hanging around, so we told dad we're going to the movies in Nevada City. We're driving ourselves. Dad's not happy, but I'm twenty-one, so he has no choice. I'll knock on the door five minutes before we leave. You come through here. Shut the wall and bring the key. Don't open the big doors, they make too much noise. There's a regular door over there," Wendy pointed. "The key will unlock it. I'll back the Jeep as close as I can, and you guys jump in the back seat."

"What if they're watching?" I asked.

"They'll never keep up with the Jeep in a limo, if either of them is drivable. I'll take you to my real mom's, and we'll tell her what's up. She's a lawyer in Sacramento. You'll be safe with her."

Wendy led us back through the garage and locked the bookcase but left the key in the lock.

"Just be ready," she said and ran up the stairs and out the door.

"Lara Croft. Should have known." Beau watched Wendy leave with admiration on his face.

I sat on the couch and looked at the view.

"I thought life was strange after I found Vera's body," I said. "That was nothing compared to this. I feel like I'm in some weird role-playing game. Any moment someone is going to come out and say 'Sorry, you lose,' and send me home."

"You wish." Beau sat next to me and dropped his arm across my shoulder. "Getting back to normal isn't going to be that simple. Nothing I believed about the world appears to be true here. Vermont is small time compared to all this." He turned to me and kissed my forehead. "You need to do anything before we leave? Write a secret message in the kitchen cabinet so the cops can find it? Collect your luggage?"

"Luggage?" I snorted. "I was drugged and abducted. I flew across America in my sweatpants and an old tee-shirt. I suppose Hammie has my driver's license and who knows what else, but I'll just have to replace that stuff when I get home. If I never see Richard Hambecker again, it will be too soon."

"Jeez, don't sugarcoat it, MacGowan." Beau laughed. "I wouldn't want to be him and meet you in a dark alley. His chances of coming away with all his parts are slim."

"Better believe it." I laid my head on his shoulder. "I missed you, Maverick, but at least you weren't worrying about where I was the last few days. Meg is probably going out of her mind. I haven't been near a working phone in days." I sat up straight. "Wait. Do you have your phone with you?"

"Sorry, Darlin', they told me not to bother bringing it. No service up here. Sounded plausible to me. I'm not married to my cell at the best of times. I figure if I need to make a call, I can find a pay phone."

"I'm here to tell you, pay phones are few and far between. I searched all over Sacramento and couldn't find one. Next time, bring it just in case." I leaned back on his shoulder. Beau may not have a cell phone, but at least I wasn't all alone in a room memorizing mug shots.

Beau dropped his hand onto my shoulder and rubbed my upper arm. He dropped his face into the crook of my neck.

"How long do you think we have?" His breath was warm on my neck, sending tingles down my spine.

"Don't know. Did you have something in mind?"

"It's been a while since I've seen you. I've missed you." He nuzzled my neck, turning my bones to liquid for about three seconds.

"Wait. You left Vermont before I did, but you didn't call and tell me where you were? So for all you knew I've been worrying about you for the last week?"

"I left a message on your machine. If you listened to your messages, you would know I was going to be away for a while."

"You didn't call my cell." It hit me hard that he hadn't wanted to talk to me personally. "You just left a message?"

"I didn't feel like arguing with you. I knew you wouldn't want me to come back here."

"You knew I'd worry?"

"Yeah, I knew you'd worry, but jeez, MacGowan, I was bored out of my mind, sitting around the house with nothing to do. I needed to get out of there, and I didn't want to fight about it. I guess this means you aren't in the mood?" He sounded hopeful.

"No, Beau, I'm not in the mood."

I was dozing when the knock came. I looked to see if anyone was coming through the door, and when no one did, I shook Beau's shoulder.

"Come on," I said, "it's time."

"They knocked?"

"Yes. Come on." I took his arm and dragged him up off the couch. He grabbed his backpack and roll of blueprints. I picked up his small valise, and we hurried to the bookcase. It swung open easily, and I pulled the key and locked the wall in place behind us. I was so excited I practically ran to the window. The limos were in the drive. They looked a little banged up, but I thought they were probably still drivable. Too bad we didn't have time to disable them.

I turned to Beau to suggest it. He was leaning on a table, obviously in pain. I moved to him and took the backpack.

"Your leg?"

He nodded.

"I'm not supposed to be walking on it. The doctor gave me a walking cast so I could get around better, take a shower, you know, do stuff. But he told me to stay off it. All this moving around hurts like hell. I don't even know where my crutches are at this point."

"I think you dropped them when you got in the limo with me." I looked out the window to see if I could see them on the ground outside, but the cars blocked much of the drive from my view.

"Don't worry about it, Bree. I'll get another pair when we get out of here."

I stood at the window and waited. I started to get nervous as the minutes ticked by. I looked back at the wall. What if someone came looking for us before the girls came for us? I looked at the key in my hand. Should I open the wall so we could pretend not to be escaping if we heard someone on the stairs? I took a step toward the hidden doorway.

"Give them some time." Beau was watching me.

"You reading my mind now?"

"I've always been able to read your mind. You just didn't know it. Wait."

"When did you ever read my mind?"

"Remember in high school, when David Shorts beat up your brother?"

I nodded. That was a day I wasn't likely ever to forget.

"You were about to say something to him and changed your mind."

"Yeah. So?"

"What you wanted to say was that he was only picking on your brother because David was gay and didn't want anyone to know. Isn't that what you were thinking?"

"Why in the world would you remember that?"

"Because that's when I first decided I was in love with you. You could have hurt David, got back at him, but you didn't because you knew that he was scared. You took care of business, and you let Davey be. That's when lust turned to love."

"You fell in love with me for doing the right thing? How ironic."

"Why ironic?"

I lifted my shoulders and let them drop. No point in trying to protect myself now.

"I usually do the wrong thing," I said.

"When?"

"Huh?" I was looking out the window again. *Where are they?*

"When have you ever done the wrong thing?" He was staring me down, daring me to tell him what I'd done.

"For one, I should never have slept with you that first time."

"Why the hell not?"

"I was drunk. Jim had just dumped me the day before. I should have said no. I should have waited."

"You regret that night?"

"Regret? No. I don't regret it, but it wasn't the right thing to do. I put both our hearts in jeopardy. There's plenty to worry about without having regrets about the good stuff. What I'm sorry for is getting you dragged into this mess."

There was movement outside. Wendy and Paris slid between the limos heading for the Jeep. I started to turn away and almost missed Guy following the girls.

"Shit."

"Quiet, he'll hear you." Beau was close behind me, looking over my shoulder. "We'll stay here until he goes back in the house. I doubt he's going with them."

We waited. I shifted from foot to foot, getting more anxious by the moment.

"Stop," Beau said in my ear. "We are not going back into the house. If push comes to shove, and they come after us through the basement, I'll block their progress, and you run. Go through the woods and hide. Try to find a house with a phone and call Fogel. He can come rescue me."

"I'm not leaving you." I said the words, but I knew they were foolish. One of us had to go for help, and Beau had a cast on his leg.

"Yes, you will. It's our only chance." We said the last together, and Beau smiled.

"I knew we'd get on the same wave length sooner or later," he said.

Wallace's henchman appeared between the limos and headed for the stairs to the second level of the house. We waited until we heard the Jeep roar to life and saw it backing down the drive alongside the limos. I trotted to the outer door and held it while Beau hobbled through.

Paris was driving the Jeep. She backed it right up to the building, and I pushed Beau toward it. Wendy was in the passenger seat with the dogs on her lap. I wondered what she had told her dad to make him believe she was taking her dogs to the movies.

"I'm locking this door. Go." I couldn't get the key in the lock, my hands were shaking so much. I took a couple of deep breaths and inserted the key. I was turning the key when Beau shouted. I looked up to see Wallace's henchman coming down the stairs two at a time.

"Shit." I abandoned the key and ran for the car. Paris was grinding the gears, trying to get the thing into first when I dove into the back seat, landing on Beau's bad leg. I heard his sharp inhale as I pushed myself off him. The Jeep was stuttering forward. We were barely moving, and the slime bag was coming around the back of the nearest limo.

"Move!" I swung myself around the roll bar into the driver's seat, Paris scrambling into the seat with Wendy.

The Jeep stalled. I hadn't gotten my foot on the clutch fast enough as Paris vacated the driver's seat.

"Bree!" Wendy and Beau were yelling, and Paris was making squeaking noises. I could see our nemesis in the rear mirror grabbing onto the rear roll bar. I jammed my foot on the clutch pedal, turned the key and rammed the gearshift into first. There was a leg coming over the back reflected in the rear view mirror. I hit the accelerator, double-clutched the thing into second and pulled out of the drive going as fast as I could. I couldn't see Guy in the mirror, so I took a quick look behind me.

"Damn."

He was standing in the back holding onto the roll cage.

# Eleven

I slammed on the brakes, sending Guy forward against the black bar. Shouting carried up the drive from the house, and I glanced back to see figures emerging from between the limos. I forced the jeep into first gear again and burned rubber. The evil henchman fell backward but managed to grab the tail of the Jeep and hang on. I accelerated through second and into third gear before I risked another look back.

Beau was pulling himself over the back of his seat as Guy tumbled over the tailgate into the little cargo area. I accelerated around a curve, sending both men flailing for something to hang onto. Paris and Wendy were clutching each other and hanging onto the dogs, trying to get the seatbelt fastened around both of them so all weren't thrown out onto the road.

A silver Sentra appeared around a curve coming toward us, causing me to slow down. No sense getting another vehicle involved in our debacle. I heard a grunt from the back, but I didn't dare turn around to see who was getting walloped on.

A flash of pink caught my eye as the Sentra passed, and a pair of startled blues eyes took us in as we passed.

"Madison!" I stomped on the brakes and glanced around in time to see her spin the rear of the Sentra around and screech to a stop behind us. She was out of the car and pulling a gun from her hip before my thought processes kicked in. Beau was under Guy, blocking blows with his forearms. They were jammed into the little cargo space, and there wasn't enough room for either of them to get a good hit on the other.

Madison came up behind the Jeep. Her hair was short now and spiked straight up. "This one?" she mouthed at me. I nodded, and she placed the barrel of the handgun up against his head. Guy froze and shifted his eyes in her direction. His hands dropped to his thighs, and I scanned for a weapon, but he appeared to be unarmed. Guess he didn't feel the need to pack while we were just hanging around the house.

Madison reached out and pulled a gun out from the small of his back, hidden by his sweatshirt. She felt around his ankles and pulled a knife from his boot on one side and a tiny handgun from the other. So much for my powers of observation.

"Why didn't you just shoot me?" Beau asked. "Wouldn't that have been a lot easier?"

"I only use weapons as a last resort. Hand-to-hand is much more …" Guy paused, "personal."

I had the feeling the word he really wanted was "satisfying," but I kept that thought to myself.

"And I had orders not to shoot anyone," he added as Madison cuffed his hands behind his back and hauled him out of the Jeep. He was pretty agile, but even so he ended up on his ass in the dirt. He got to his feet without saying anything, which surprised me.

"Are you all okay?" I asked Beau and the two girls. Paris and Wendy nodded. Wendy was trying to unfasten the seatbelt, and I thought she wanted nothing more than to get out of that Jeep and never get in again. I hit the release button for her, and the girls sprang apart and tumbled out onto the road.

"I'm fine." Beau climbed back over the back of the seat and propped his leg up. "But I think I'd better get this leg re-casted. Does she know she looks like a pink hedgehog?"

His lip was bleeding, and he had a bruise on his cheek and another on his forehead. His cast was in worse shape.

"She thinks she's a shape-shifting alien. I don't think looking like a hedgehog is going to faze her. Oh, hey, that sounds like a pun. Get it? Shape-shifting, phasing?"

"There's something wrong with you." Beau shot me a disgusted look. "Seriously wrong."

While Madison locked Guy in the back of her car, I got out and stood on the road. My heart was racing, and I leaned against the Jeep, which wasn't all that easy as there was more empty space than there was metal. I leaned into the back seat, giving Beau the once over.

"We'd better get you to the hospital," I said. "You're a mess. Are you sure you're all right?" I dabbed at the blood on the corner of his mouth.

"That hurts." Beau jerked his head away from my touch. "Nothing irreparable, but I'd rather not have to fight off any more bad guys for you."

Madison appeared at the side of the car, speaking into her cell phone. She flipped it closed and looked at Beau. "You should get out of here. Take him to the hospital in Grass Valley. I'll deal with this guy."

"Be careful, you're outnumbered if they show up from the cabin."

"I've got back-up coming, and Hambecker is in their camp, although to be truthful, I'm not really sure whose side he's on. We've been saying he's FBI, but I don't rightly know who he's with. The intel is he's an agent of some sort, but he doesn't show up on the rosters in any of the regular agencies."

"MIB," I said, but I didn't really believe it.

"MIB?" she asked.

"Don't tell me you've never seen *Men in Black*. It's a classic."

"Oh. Yeah. I've seen it. Wasn't thinking about movies, so when you said MIB it threw me for a loop. I doubt it's space aliens." She barked out a short laugh. "But a secret agency? I'd believe that."

The sound of screaming engines came to us from up the road. We looked at each other for a moment.

"Go," Madison said. "Get out of here now."

I turned to the girls still huddled together on the road.

"Paris! Wendy!"

They turned to look at me, eyes wide. I hoped I had never looked that vulnerable.

"Get in the Jeep. Drive Beau to the hospital. Stay there until I get there. OK?"

"Are you nuts?" Madison asked. "You're going, too."

"It's me they're after. If I don't go, these three have a better chance of making it to the hospital, and I'm not leaving you here alone."

I turned back to the girls who were standing with their mouths hanging open.

"Now!" I hadn't meant to shout, but damn it, they needed to move.

They moved. The Jeep was roaring out of sight when two snowmobiles and a four-wheeler zoomed into sight along the dirt road. I should have remembered the snowmobiles could run without snow. Madison had angled her car across the road so they couldn't easily pursue the Jeep, and we stood on either side of it. They would have to go through us to catch the Jeep, but I didn't think they'd try. It was me Wallace really wanted. They could have me packed up and out of there before Beau alerted the sheriff's department.

Hambecker and Moose were riding the four-wheeler, and I couldn't see faces under the helmets riding the ski machines. I doubted I would recognize them; there were a bunch of people at the cabin I hadn't been introduced to. Hambecker headed straight for me, but I held my ground. Giving Beau time to get to the hospital was my highest priority.

The ATV skidded to a halt in front of me, and the two men were off it and on me in a heartbeat. Moose produced a set of metal cuffs and secured my hands together in front of my body while Hambecker held me. The other two guys were at a standoff with Madison as she was armed. One of them had produced a handgun but looked hesitant to use it. Madison, on the other hand, was planted gun in hand, feet wide, arms straight out, aiming at the thug. She had never looked less like a shape shifter than she did right now. She'd transformed into a pink-haired Olivia Benson, and I'd been standing right there.

My guess was that if shots were fired, Madison would hit her target, and the rent-a-thug would miss. He must have thought that, too, because he was looking at his partner with panic on his face.

"Bree." Hambecker's voice was quiet in my ear. "If I let you escape, it'll blow my cover. So sit tight, OK? I promise to keep you safe."

He handed me over to Moose and headed toward the others. I glanced at the four-wheeler and wondered if it was possible to drive it with my hands cuffed together. It took me about two seconds to figure out that I'd crash if I tried, so I switched my gaze to the rental car. I'd driven a car handcuffed before. That was do-able. Not the safest way to go, but definitely do-able.

Moose's attention was on Hambecker, and his grasp on me was relaxed. He didn't expect me to break away. I didn't give a rat's ass about anyone's cover. He and Moose could rot in hell as far as I was concerned. I stepped away from Moose. He took a step toward Hambecker, who was talking quietly to Madison. Madison hadn't even twitched. She stood exactly as she had from the beginning, her sights on the guy with the gun.

"Madison, you're my hero," I said, but not loud enough to distract her.

I took another step away from Moose toward the car. He didn't notice. I turned and walked to the driver's side door. I looked around. I could have been invisible for all the attention I was getting. Good.

Guy was still in the back seat, hands cuffed behind his back. Madison must have engaged the child locks on the rear doors, or he would have been long gone. Should I take him with me or turn him loose? If I turned him loose, it might tip the scales away from Madison; if I took him with me there was a chance he could foul me up in some way.

I opened the driver's door and popped the lock. I was beyond caring. Madison was a Fed. She could handle herself, and Hambecker wouldn't let any real harm come to her. I hoped. I opened the back door and dragged Guy out of the car.

"What are you doing? I don't want out of the car. I might get shot."

"Saving myself. You're on your own. Good luck." I pushed him away from the car, slammed the passenger door, and slid into the driver's seat, hitting the locks before he could get back in. The car was standard. That made things a lot more interesting. Good thing I'd kicked the bad guy out. I was going to need to concentrate.

I shoved in the clutch and started the car. With my right hand on the stick shift my left hand couldn't reach the steering wheel. Great. I put the car in reverse, let out the clutch, and gingerly backed around, careful not to take Madison out with the rear of the car.

I shifted into first, got my hands on the wheel and pulled the car forward onto the road going the opposite way. I was heading to the hospital. As I started forward, a fleet of black cars swarmed up the road. After them came a couple of forlorn sheriff's cruisers with lights flashing and sirens blaring. They didn't block my way, so I inched past, risking a glance in the rearview as I went. Hammie and Moose had completely disappeared. I stopped the car and turned around, but it wasn't my imagination. They were completely gone. The four-wheeler stood where I left it, Madison was still planted with gun leveled and the other two thugs had their hands held high. I couldn't see where the thug's gun had gone, but I assumed it was on the ground at Madison's feet.

As I started forward again the armada came to a halt, and almost immediately the area was crawling with agents. Time for me to be gone. I eased the car forward and drove down the hill like a little old lady. It took forever for me to reach the freeway, and driving the interstate in handcuffs gave me the heebie-jeebies. It wasn't long before I reached the hospital exit and finally pulled into the emergency parking lot. I slid into a space next to the Jeep, pulled the keys out of the ignition, and walked through the sliding doors into the emergency waiting room. The handcuffs made me feel conspicuous, like a criminal, and I was happy to see Wendy and Paris huddled in a corner.

"Do you need us to remove those cuffs?" The receptionist sounded bored, like people with cuffs walked into the emergency room every day.

"Uh, yeah. That'd be great."

"You've got to register, then." She handed me a clipboard and a pen. Turns out writing with your hands in cuffs is tricky when you're trying to hold a clipboard. I set it on the counter and had better luck holding the papers still with my left arm while I wrote with my right. I skipped over the part about how I got the injury. I had my doubts that they'd remove them if they knew some kind of special agent put them on me.

"How did you get that bruise on your cheek? That's a doozey."

"Had a minor fender bender. It's nothing."

"Have a seat. It'll be a few minutes."

"Bree!" Wendy jumped up and threw her arms around me. "We were afraid you wouldn't be able to get away. I'm so glad you're here."

"What's this?" She grabbed my arm. "How did you get cuffs on you?"

"Richard Hambecker. Where's Beau? Getting a new cast on?"

"They were giving him the third degree about how he got all banged up." Paris patted the seat beside her. Wendy and I sat down, our backs to the room.

"But why did Richard cuff you?" asked Paris.

"Didn't want me to leave, I guess." I decided not to blow his cover in front of the girls. "But I took off anyway. Didn't want to stick around for the firefight."

"Firefight?" Wendy looked at me wide-eyed.

"Madison Truefellow, I don't know if you know her, she's the woman who showed up and locked Guy in her car. She had her gun out ready to mow down anyone who moved, and I decided that was as good a time as any to take my leave."

"Wow." Wendy looked shell shocked. "That must have been frightening."

"You said the doctor was giving Beau the third degree. What did he say?" I was curious about how Beau would play this, kidnap *vs.* accident victim.

"Said he jumped into the back of the Jeep while Wendy was driving. She got startled and slammed on the brake, and he got banged up. Don't think they totally bought it. Looks too much like he was beat up."

"We were in with him, but they took him into x-ray, and we came out to get something to eat. They said they'd let us know when he got back."

"Bree MacGowan?"

I turned around to see a male nurse dressed in blue with a clipboard in his hand. I got up and went to him.

"I'm Bree."

He looked down at my wrists, and his lips twitched.

"Nice bracelets," he said. "Who gave you those?"

"Nobody important. I'd sure like to get rid of them though."

"We're here to serve." He swung around and led me into the treatment area where he sat me on a bed and told me to wait.

After about fifteen minutes I decided I was tired of sitting and rested my head on the pillow. I was on the brink of sleep when I heard a gurney wheeled into the next cubicle, which wouldn't have interrupted the sleep process except for a familiar voice.

"You're very good with your hands." Beau's voice was clear from the next cubicle.

"I've been doing this for a while. Hold still."

This was too good. I pushed myself up off the bed and walked out into the hall, around the glass partition and into Beau's room. Beau was lying on the gurney, eyes half shut, not from his injuries. Painkillers, I thought. A hospital tech was wrapping Beau's leg in plaster. She was alternating strips of pink, black and green.

"Wow," I said, "that's one colorful cast."

The tech jumped and dropped a swath of black plaster onto the floor. Beau looked up and smiled. "Bree, you found me. Come here and give me a kiss. I'm feeling very good."

"Can't," I said. "I've got to go back and have my cuffs removed."

"Don't bother," said a voice behind me. "I can do that in here. Didn't know you two knew each other."

"She's my girl." Beau's voice warmed me for a moment until I remembered the cuffs and the broken leg wouldn't be easy to explain away, besides the fact he was high on painkillers and never talked that way about me normally.

"A woman in cuffs and a guy with a broken leg. Actually, no. A woman in cuffs and a guy with a broken leg in a cast that's been totaled. You know what? I'm not even going to ask. In fact, I don't want to know. We're keeping the paperwork separate on this one." He pulled out a key and released me from the cuffs.

"I thought you were going to cut them off."

"We tell people that for effect, but we've got handcuff keys here. You'd be surprised how often people get themselves locked into them and lose the keys. Sign here."

I signed my release papers and pulled up a chair next to Beau. Wendy and Paris could wait in the lobby.

"Feeling pretty good, aren't you?" I took Beau's hand and watched the tech finishing up the neon cast.

"Yep. Nothing hurts at the moment." Beau smiled at me. "But don't worry, I know I'm going to be in a world of hurt when the drugs wear off. You still owe me a kiss."

I leaned over and kissed him gently on the cheek. Painkillers or no, his mouth was bruised and swollen, and I couldn't believe that it wouldn't hurt if I touched it.

"Right." The tech gathered up the trash left over from the re-casting. "That should be set by the time we get the paperwork ready to be signed. Hang out for a while, and someone will be back to sign you out."

Beau nodded and closed his eyes. I leaned back in my chair. The muscles in my neck were complaining again. My face hurt, too. I needed heat and a really good massage, both of which I could possibly get here, but it would mean checking back in and waiting and God knew what else. I'd be okay. Maybe I could get Beau to give me one of his painkillers.

I sat dozing beside Beau until the lady with the discharge papers and a computer on a cart came rolling into the room. Beau was still asleep, so I answered the questions and signed the papers while she entered information into the computer. A nurse showed up with a wheelchair just as the computer was being wheeled away, so I roused Beau and helped him into the chair and rolled him out into the waiting room where Wendy and Paris were talking to Fogel.

Fogel must have caught sight of us from the corner of his eye, because he swung around and jogged over.

"My God, Bree, I've been worried about you. You wouldn't believe the uproar your disappearance has caused. I've got Brooks calling me every couple of hours. Steve Leftsky is pretending to attend a law enforcement convention in Sacramento while he haunts me and walks around the river looking under rocks for your cold body. Tom Maverick calls more than Brooks does. Says his wife is beside herself with worry, but I think he's just as concerned."

"But you knew where I was, or at least who I was with, didn't you? Couldn't you assure everyone that I was in good hands?"

"I assumed you were with someone safe, but I didn't know who it was or where they'd taken you until I got a call from Madison Truefellow alerting me you were in Sacramento. Today, of course, I got a call for backup from her just a little while ago. I sent backup and headed down here to make sure you're okay. The girls there," he nodded to Paris and Wendy, "told me you were handcuffed but that you weren't harmed. That true?"

"I'm all right. I can't say the same about Richard Hambecker. I poisoned the whole household trying to get away."

Fogel reached down and shook Beau's hand.

"Forgive me for ignoring you, Beau, I didn't know you were back in California. Were you in on the Bree search, too?"

"I didn't know Bree was missing. A day after we flew home I was approached by a guy who wanted me to do some stonework. I told him I wouldn't be able to do any actual work for several weeks, but he said come out and do the planning. So I did. I had no idea I was a captive until Bree came to rescue me. Dense, huh?"

Fogel turned his attention back to me.

"So where have you been? No, that I can't guess." He glanced over to where Wendy and Paris were collecting their trash.

"Senator Wallace's house in Sacramento."

Fogel looked like he wanted to slap a hand to his forehead.

"God, that man has nerve. He must think we're stupid," he said. "We've heard from the wife's lawyer. She was going to divorce him."

"He's trying to get me to finger a couple of parolees for his wife's murder. Tried to appeal to my sense of community, my friends. He grabbed Beau, and then he tried to bribe me. I don't have any proof, but I'm pretty sure he killed his wife."

"I'm going to take you over to the office to make a statement. Then I'm keeping you there until the situation at the Wallace cabin is resolved."

Paris drove the Jeep, Wendy drove Madison's rental car, and Beau and I rode in Fogel's squad car. Fogel wasn't taking any chances on us disappearing between the hospital and the station. Wendy and Paris decided it was in their interest to stick with us until Fogel thought it was safe for them to go home—their own homes, not back to Wallace's.

Fogel sat me down with a female officer in the squad room while Beau was led down the hall to a conference room. I thought it was kind of funny that they separated us, but it probably was standard operating procedure.

It took forever for me to tell the entire story. I started with finding Lily Wallace and continued from there into being abducted from my home. I could tell the officer didn't completely believe Hambecker existed, and Moose was a big question mark in her mind, as well. She kept harping back to his association with the FBI, but I knew less than nothing about him. I figured at least half of what he told me was a lie, and Moose, too. I felt a little sad about the loss of the blue shoes and matching dress. I really liked those shoes.

I must have spent a little too much time describing the shoes, because the officer was looking at me like I was off my rocker. I got back to the point and finished my story, ending at the hospital. She printed a copy from her computer and gave it to me to sign while she went to check in with Fogel. I could tell she didn't like me. Everything about her, from the look on her face to the way she held herself when she walked away, told me that she didn't approve.

I started to read, and the copy editor/reporter in me compelled me to correct grammar along with the details of my account. I scratched out "black dress" and wrote in "blue dress and matching shoes." I noted that the limo was bulletproof and soundproof and that a passenger could be locked in. I described the pictures of the two men Wallace was trying to frame. When she returned I was describing the cabin and the road that led to it.

The officer looked at the corrections and sighed.

"Are those really necessary?" she asked.

"Only if accuracy is important. But I'll make the changes if you want. I'm good with a keyboard."

"Sorry, I'm not giving up my keyboard to anybody." She sat and made the changes. I watched carefully, making sure she got the details right, and I re-read the whole thing before signing it.

"You know," I said, looking up at her, "you don't really need to put a comma …"

The look she was giving me would freeze a polar bear. Maybe a lesson in grammar wasn't really appropriate right now.

She led me back into Fogel's office and left me there while Fogel read my report. I sat quietly watching him scan the document. It was about five minutes before he looked up.

"You know what I find really interesting about firsthand witness accounts? The different way in which people see and describe the world. Beau says, and I quote, 'Bree got us out of there.' You, however, go into a detailed description of how you told Wendy and Paris to drive Beau to the hospital, what kind of gun Ms. Truefellow was holding, how many people were on snow machines, and how many were on the ATV. It fascinates me."

"I'm a reporter. I can't help myself." I shrugged.

"I gathered. Mary told me that you about made her crazy with your corrections to your statement. Beau glanced over his and signed on the dotted line. Like I said, people fascinate me." Fogel smiled, his eyes crinkling at the corners. He looked a little greyer around the temples than when I'd left California the last time.

"You need a vacation," I said. "Get away from the job."

"What I need a vacation from is you getting yourself tangled up in this murder. I swear all this has taken ten years off my life. I'll feel like I'm on vacation once we get you home again."

"Yeah." I sighed. "I'll feel like I'm on vacation, too. I miss my dogs."

Beau hobbled in on a new set of crutches and sat in the chair beside me.

"Where'd you get the crutches?" I asked.

"They keep these things around, apparently." He smiled a lopsided smile.

"You're not feeling any pain are you?"

"Nope. None at all. I'm hoping I've got enough painkiller to keep me happy until we get home again. I can't imagine five hours on a plane without access to them. Brutal."

The phone rang, and Fogel answered while Beau melted into his chair and I stared out the window. It had started to rain, cold early December rain. If this was Vermont it would have been snow. Now that I was in relative safety, I was free to really miss home. I knew my animals would be well cared for. I boarded my neighbor's horses, and we traded services freely, caring for each other's animals on a regular basis. I wasn't worried about them, but I missed their company. I'd just gotten reacquainted after a really long absence when I'd been snatched. Thinking about home got me thinking about my bedroom, sparsely furnished but full of light with an old wooden frame that held the mattress so high off the floor that I needed a stepstool to get into bed. The beautifully carved head board, the soft mattress. I hoped Annabelle hadn't used it as a litter box again.

"Shit!" Fogel's exclamation jolted me awake and back into the present. He hung up the phone and looked across at me. "Wallace disappeared along with Hambecker and the guy you call Moose. We picked up some of Wallace's thugs, but they're all claiming they haven't seen Wallace for weeks. We've lost him."

"Hambecker and Moose, too?" I was disappointed. Okay, they'd flown, but with Wallace? They were the good guys, weren't they? Hell, this wasn't the first time I'd ever been wrong.

"Who's going to tell Paris and Wendy?"

Fogel looked at me with eyebrows raised.

"Paris is Hambecker's girlfriend, and Wendy is Wallace's daughter. They deserve to know." As I talked I got the sinking feeling that I'd be the one telling the girls. I didn't know how Wendy would feel. Wallace was her father, after all. She might be glad he'd gotten away, but poor Paris. How do you tell a girl her boyfriend skipped town with a murderer? There was no easy way to break the news.

Fogel was still looking at me.

"Oh, no," I said. "Not me. You've got policewomen who are trained to do this kind of thing. No way I'm going to break the bad news."

"Come with me then. It helps to have a familiar face when news like this is received. They won't feel quite so abandoned."

I followed Fogel out of his office and down to the lower floor where we'd left Wendy and Paris in a waiting room with comfortable couches and vending machines, obviously not a room for criminals. They were sitting across from each other at a table playing cards and eating animal crackers.

Fogel grabbed a chair and turned it around so he could sit backwards on it, his arms resting on the plastic back. I slid into a chair across from him, snagging a cracker and resting my elbows on the table. Wendy looked at us and set her cards on the table face up.

"My father disappeared, didn't he?" she said. Fogel nodded. "Damn it! This happens every time something unpleasant or illegal happens. All of a sudden he's gone. He must pay his staff a bundle to lie for him." She started gathering the cards and shoving them roughly into their case. "He's got too much power for his own good. He gets away with everything. My mom's right. He's no damn good."

"What about Richard?" Paris asked quietly. Her voice shook slightly, and I thought she knew the answer. "Will he be coming here to get us? I know the limo was totaled, and we have the Jeep."

I shook my head, and she looked down, but when she looked back up her face was determined.

"It's not like I didn't know he wasn't going to stick. For one thing, he was way too old for me. He's, like, your age, isn't he Bree?"

"Um, yeah. I guess so." Since when was thirty old? "Actually, I think he was even older than I am." Take that, Hambecker.

"See? Too old for me. I'm going back to college with Wendy. I bet they'll let me back in."

"Paris, we're on winter break. You haven't even missed anything yet." Wendy looked at Paris and rolled her eyes.

"See, I told you they'd let me back in. Come on, Wendy, I want to get back to town." The girls gathered their purses and jackets. Wendy hugged me goodbye.

"Well, they're going to be okay," I said as they left. "Nothing like youth for bouncing back. What about us? You going to let us go home now, too?"

"Not until you've got tickets and an escort. I'm not taking any chances with you two."

Fogel finally agreed that we'd probably be safe if we stayed in the Law Enforcement Convention's headquarters hotel. He gave us a ride to Sacramento, got us checked in and wished us luck. I noticed him talking to a cop and gesturing in our direction as we got on the elevator. Not that the place wasn't crawling with police officers, but I had the feeling he was making sure that Sacramento's finest knew we were here.

Beau collapsed on the bed and fell asleep immediately. I didn't know if it was exhaustion or the pain pills, but he'd earned a little oblivion. Time for me to get cleaned up a little. I gathered all the little bottles of shampoo, conditioner and body wash and ran the water hot. I was going to stand in the water until the memories of the past few days were soaked out of me.

There was quiet knocking on the door as I was coming out of the shower.

"Hang on," I whispered through the door and pulled on the same dirty clothes I'd been wearing for days. I stepped out into the hall to find Steve Leftsky leaning against the wall.

"What were you doing in there? Took you forever to open the door."

"Beau's sleeping, and I didn't want to wake him. What in the world are you doing in California?" I asked him even though I knew.

"Officially, I'm attending the law enforcement convention. Unofficially, Brooks sent me out here to help find you. I haven't even seen the inside of the conference center, but now that you found me, I can go to the banquet tonight. The food's the best part anyway. You can go as my date."

"You just got Shirl back. I don't think that's a good idea. What if she asked you about it?"

"It won't be an issue."

"Why not?"

"She broke up with me again. Said if I took this assignment, she was leaving for good."

"Will you never learn? If you had turned it down, she would have stuck with you forever."

"I couldn't turn it down. It was me or no one. I've known you since grade school. I can't spend my life not doing what I know to be the right thing because it might upset her. She should understand. If she was right for me, she would understand. Come to the banquet with me. I don't want to be one of the losers who couldn't get a date."

"Okay. I'll come, provided I can get away from Beau, Fogel and the FBI."

The big problem with going to the banquet was my lack of anything to wear—nothing to wear, no wallet, money or ID. How the heck was I going to get on an airplane without any ID? Beau solved the money problem by lending me his credit cards.

"Go," he said. "Go and spend my money. I can't do anything with it."

So I shopped. New underclothes, black dress and shoes. Then more new underclothes, the comfortable kind, along with sweat pants to sleep in, jeans and long sleeved tee-shirts for the trip home. When I got back to the hotel, I called Fogel and asked him how he was going to convince TSA to let me through security with no ID. He said he'd check into it and get back to me.

I barely had enough time to change and swipe on mascara and lipstick. The black dress looked good. Beau roused himself long enough to wolf whistle at me before smiling and going back to sleep. I was doing the last-minute adjustments when there was a tap at my door.

Steve let out a low whistle when I let him into the room. He walked in and did a circuit around me like I was a show dog or something. I frowned at him as he stood in front of me again, taking in the package.

"What are you scowling at me for? You are looking good. I'm thinking I might have to change my personal rules about making moves on my female friends. Yow!"

"I am not sleeping with you, Steve, so you can just put that thought right back in your pants, and I don't appreciate being treated like a prize poodle being judged on its conformation. It's okay for you to compliment me, but after that you have to ignore the fact I'm the hottest girl in the room and go back to treating me like your buddy. Otherwise, I'm going to have to kick your ass."

"Jeez, all right. I was just appreciating the dress, that's all. Apparently that's not kosher, so I'll stop."

We rode the elevator down to the third floor, and Steve took my arm as we walked into the banquet hall. I got the distinct feeling that if he wasn't going to be spending the night with me, he was going to be darn well certain that no one else would either.

We found the table we were assigned to, and I dropped the little rhinestone bag holding my room keycard and rhubarb lipstick on my chair. Then Steve and I headed for the group gathered at the side of the room. It was pitifully obvious that we were in a room full of cops. The percentage of shaved heads alone would have given it away, but cops also have a way of holding themselves, which I figure comes from the police academy.

There were a few long-haired slouchers sitting around a table, so obviously undercover cops it was painful. They had obviously managed to overcome their cadet training. We pushed past the group and stood in line at the bar. While we were waiting for the bartender to pop the tops off our beers, I made a game of guessing which of the women were cops and which were wives and girlfriends.

There was a pretty brunette who kept pushing her curls out of her face and was so awkward in her heels that I figured she had to be a uniform. The blonde in a red sparkly sheath, hanging onto the arm of a muscled cop, I took for a girlfriend. And the redhead in jeans sitting with the longhaired guys had to be undercover herself.

Being neither wife nor girlfriend should have made me feel out of place, but I felt pretty damn good. For one thing I was in a room full of cops, so nobody was going to abduct tonight. For another, to judge from the looks I was getting, I cleaned up pretty good. I smiled at the bartender. It was fine evening.

I took my beer and headed back to the table, nearly spilling my beer on a guy who leaned back in his chair right in front of me to shout at his buddy.

"You owe me ninety-nine cent," he called as I clipped his chair, juggling my beer and glass. "Oops, sorry miss."

"What?" His buddy called.

"Ninety-nine cent. You owe me."

"There's no such thing as ninety-nine cent."

"What the hell you talkin' about? You owe me a buck."

"Its ninety nine cents, numb nuts. There's no such thing as ninety-nine cent."

I skirted his chair, leaving them to argue across the room like a couple of teenagers. I put my beer on the table and picked the clutch up off my chair, but Steve caught my arm before I could sit down.

"Come on," he said. "There's something you've got to see in the other room." He steered me away from my beer and through the tables to a door leading to another conference room. In the middle of the floor was a shiny new black-and-white police cruiser. It looked like a modified SUV with a fancy bumper, almost like a cowcatcher, on the front. Steve pulled me over to it and opened the driver's side door.

"Get in."

I slid under the wheel and looked at the dash. It was like being in the cockpit of a private jet. Steve slid in the passenger side. Everything looked high tech and state of the art.

"It's the new thing," Steve said. "A company called Carbon Motors designed it. They want to market it to police agencies across the country. So instead of driving re-purposed Crown Vics, we'd all have these custom built jobbies. Cool, huh?"

"What are all these things?" I motioned to the dash. There was an LCD screen built into it. "That's not a TV, is it?"

"No, it's not a TV, it's a computer. This thing has all the latest stuff. It automatically runs the number of every plate the camera in the front bumper picks up. You can even launch a GPS tracker at a speeding car so you don't have to give chase. That's a big deal. It doesn't happen much in Vermont, but in other places high-speed chases end in crashes. Wonder what that will do to the popularity of the website devoted to police chases? Anyway, the front of this sucker is bulletproof."

"Are you telling me regular cop cars aren't bulletproof? How come I didn't know that?" I was feeling pretty stupid. Considering Tom was captain at the barracks and Steve was a patrol officer, you'd think I'd know more about it.

"No, most patrol cars aren't bulletproof. What I wouldn't give for one of these."

"Have you ever been shot at in your car?"

"Well, no, but it would be nice to know that no one could pick me off in my car. It worries me sometimes."

We slid out of the car, and I took a look around it. It was like a glossy new toy.

"What would it take to get you one of these?"

"You can't buy just one. They only sell them in fleets. That's the only way they could make the price comparable to a re-purposed Crown Vic."

"Jeez. That's too bad. You guys should have these."

"You could write a letter to the guy in charge for us. Put in a good word."

"Because Lord knows I'm in good with the guy in charge. Bree? Bree who? Keep dreaming, Steve."

We wandered back into the banquet room where it looked like they were getting ready to serve dinner. I sat down and took a drink of my beer. It seemed strange to be swigging beer wearing a fancy dress, but it was what everyone was doing. At least the cops.

The servers started bringing meals to the tables near the door, and the other occupants of our table sat down and introduced themselves. Three couples, two married, one not. I forgot most of their names the minute after I heard them except for the redhead who sat next to me. She was the undercover cop I'd seen earlier. Her name was Meg. My best friend's name. I immediately started missing home.

"What's the matter?" asked the redheaded Meg sitting next to me.

"Nothing," I said. "My best friend's name is Meg, and I haven't seen her in a while. I probably should lay off the beer."

"Nah, have more. That way you'll be in too much pain to miss her tomorrow." She laughed, joyful and free. I smiled.

"You have a great laugh," I said. "It's contagious."

"Need a sense of humor in my job. Something like ninety percent of undercover cops are guys. If I couldn't laugh, I'd go nuts."

"I know what you mean." I looked at her with interest. "But I bet you're not bored much."

"Nah, almost never bored." She laughed again.

"I'm going to get another beer," she said. "You want one?"

"Sure."

I turned to Steve.

"Sorry, girl talk."

"That's fine. I'm glad you're enjoying yourself."

A hand dropped onto my shoulder, and I looked up to see Steve's Shirl standing over me.

"I think you're sitting in my seat."

Next to me Steve was stammering.

"Shirl? What are you-?"

"Oh. Hey, Shirl. I was saving it for you." I grabbed my little beaded bag and vacated the chair. She was wearing a red dress designed to catch eyes, backless, low cut and so tight you could see every pore in her body. Yowsers. Leftsky didn't have a chance.

"Glad to see you aren't missing anymore, Bree. I think everybody in the Upper Valley was worrying."

"Thanks. It's good to be found. See you later, Steve."

Steve started to get up, but I shook my head at him. I wasn't getting in Shirl's way. I wanted to still be un-missing tomorrow.

"You're back early." Beau was lying propped on the bed watching a cop show on TV.

"Yeah, well, Shirl showed up, and I thought it might be a good idea to bow out."

"Shirl showed up? You mean like showed up from Vermont?"

"As far as I can tell." I hung the black dress in the closet and slipped on an oversized T-shirt.

"That new?" Beau asked. "Don't think I've seen that before."

I joined him on the bed and punched up my pillow.

"I picked it up today. You paid for it."

"I've got good taste." He slid a hand along my thigh.

"Yep, you do. Want me to put it back on?" I dropped a kiss on his chin.

"Nope." He pulled me into a kiss that melted my knees. "But I think you could lose the T-shirt."

So I did.

I woke to more tapping at the door. Beau was asleep beside me, so I slid out of bed and pulled on my new sweats. I almost opened the door without looking through the peephole, but I caught myself and looked to see Steve's face sporting the biggest smile I'd ever seen.

I stepped out into the hall. "So what's up? You look like you just won the lottery."

"Shirl asked me to marry her."

I threw my arms around him. "Steve, that's so great! She flew out here to propose? That's wild."

"Yeah, I guess her mother told her she was being unreasonable. She thought about it for a while and realized her mom was right. So she bought a ticket and flew out. If you hadn't been found, she was going to help me look. But you were here, so she proposed instead."

"That's great. I can't think of anything but crappy clichés. I'm glad you're happy." I hugged him again and headed back to bed.

"What was that about?" Beau asked. "You were squealing in the hall."

"I wasn't squealing. Shirl asked Steve to marry him. He wanted me to know."

"It's about time, although I doubt the drama is over."

# Twelve

Madison drove us to the airport. She was tall, thin and brunette today. I didn't think the look was quite right for her, but hey, it wasn't my life. For all I knew, she'd be short, blue haired and plump by the end of the day.

She offered me her hand when Beau and I were on the sidewalk.

"No hard feelings?" she asked.

"God, no," I said. "You saved my skin. Come visit Vermont sometime. You could let your hair grow out to its natural color for a while, rediscover the real you."

"Thanks for the invite, but I'm not sure you want to see an alien shape shifter's natural color. It's a little startling to see a woman with transparent hair."

Beau decided getting home was the key thing, and he sprang for first class tickets, the only seats that were available to us at short notice. I couldn't help but wonder how much influence the painkillers had had on that decision, but I wasn't complaining. I was more than ready to go home.

The trip was uneventful. Fogel had taken care of the ID problem, and we flew from Sacramento to Manchester, New Hampshire, not nonstop, but at least we didn't have to change planes. Tom and Meg were at the airport without their kids for a change. Meg told me later that they weren't sure what kind of shape we would be in and didn't want to alarm the younger kids. Not that it mattered to me. I slept through both car rides and the flight.

My homecoming was all I expected it to be. The beagle, boxer, lab cross and Irish wolfhound all tried to get into my lap at once. The Chihuahua completely ignored me and sat behind the cat, who hissed at me and unsheathed her claws.

"All right, Annabelle, I know you're mad at me for leaving you again, but it wasn't my choice, believe me. As for you, you little jumping bean," I picked up Beans and held him up to my face. He growled at me. "Listen, you aren't even really my responsibility. Quit with the tough dog act. I'll take you to Beau's house tomorrow."

Only Lucky treated me normally. When I'd settled in and made my way out to see how everything in the barn was doing, he looked up from his hay, snorted and went back to eating. He seemed to enjoy the rubdown I gave him and puffed his breath onto my neck, but it was more like a "nice to have you back" versus the "Oh my God where have you been" I got from the dogs or the "I'm never going to forgive you" that Annabelle greeted me with.

I walked through the side yard around to where the chicken house stood. Counting the chickens was a homecoming ritual for me. My chickens were pretty good at self-preservation, but you never knew when a fox or coyote would sneak in and grab one. My chickens were a constant source of vexation for me. I loved them, they made me laugh, and like all my animals, I was insanely attached to them. The problem was that I kept chickens partially because I liked having fresh eggs. I have twenty-eight chickens, but lately I'm lucky to find even one egg a day.

The phone was ringing when I woke the next morning. I figured I'd be answering a lot of calls until the news of where I'd been got around, and life went back to normal.

"Hey, MacGowan! Get your butt down here. You slept all the way home, and I want to hear all about what happened." It was Meg.

"I'll be down in a little bit. I desperately need a shower, and then I need to drop Beanie off at Beau's. Give me an hour."

I drove into Meg's drive almost an hour to the minute after I hung up the phone. Beans was still in my lap, as when I got to Beau's he wasn't there. Not knowing when Beau would be home, I didn't leave the little guy. He was still young, and I didn't trust him not to pee on the rug, the bed, the couch or the chair. Besides, he wasn't used to going solo.

I carried Beans through the flying snow to the back door. Meg's dogs surged around me as I stepped into the mudroom, and I put Beans on the floor. Beans was used to Meg's house and ran off through the kitchen with a pack of dogs in tow. I kicked off my boots, hung my jacket on a peg and made my way through the remaining dogs into the kitchen.

"Wow! My God, Meg, how did you do that?" The sheet rock we'd started to hang before my absence from the project had been covered with beautiful bronze tiles that were embossed in patterns. The new ceiling gave height and light to the kitchen, creating the illusion of a bigger room. Meg was at the sink, rinsing glasses and stacking them in the drainer

"Jeez, this must have cost you a fortune," I said. "When did you decide to go with a metal ceiling?"

"I don't know, I guess when we found all that old metal under the Homasote, but it's not real embossed bronze or anything. It's molded plastic, painted with metallic paint. It was pretty inexpensive compared with, say, real metal tiles." She laughed. "I think they look pretty good, if I say so myself."

"Looks fab. What's Tom think?"

"He likes it. It was a little too much work in his mind, but I think it was worth it. Forget the ceiling. Tell me what happened to you. I had to run a story written by Lucy in the paper and listen to her yak about how I'd have to hire her back if you didn't show up soon. Dirty little ..."

"Backstabbing Howe," I finished with her. Not that all Howes were like Lucy. It's just what we'd called her for as long as I could remember.

"Spill."

So I told my story, front to back, including the identity of the dead woman and the mysterious Richard Hambecker and his disappearance. A gambit of emotions ran across her face as I talked, and she got more and more serious as I got to the end.

"The senator got away? He murdered his wife and got away?"

"As far as I know. I haven't heard any noises about him showing up back in Sacramento. My bet is Mexico. Easy access."

"And Richard Hambecker?" The look she shot me made me squirm. Meg could always read my mind. "Do you think he headed to Mexico, too?"

"No. Somehow I think he's cut his losses and moved back into the dark recesses of whatever agency he came out of, the identity of which remains a mystery. I'm thinking not the FBI, because that's where Madison hails from, and she swears those boys were not with her."

"You really can't remember Moose's real name? That's strange."

"I'm pretty sure he told me, but I just can't remember. I'm blaming it on the drugs. I'm sure being sedated for hours on end must have affected my memory."

"Richard admitted to sedating you? Why would he do that? You could sue him for all sorts of things, if you ever saw him again."

"He always seemed like an unlikely thug—or agent, whichever. He was nice to me. He seemed like the kind of guy who's naturally nice to people in general, but he had this hard edge, too. Self-preservation, I think. The ability to do what needed to be done, even if it was distasteful to him."

"Well, I don't like him. Anybody who can drug a woman and drag her all the way across the country is not okay in my book, especially when it's my best friend he's abducted."

"How did you even find out I was gone? It's not like I called everybody up and announced I'd been abducted."

"Max called. He stopped by to see to his horses and noticed the dogs acting strangely. He checked in the house and called Tom when you weren't there. Tom called me. He was hoping you'd decided to go away for a couple of days or something and forgot to tell Max, like you'd ever leave your animals without making sure you had them taken care of."

"He was just hopeful. He would rather think I'd neglected my animals than think I'd been abducted. It's a natural response."

"Then there was the mad flurry of activity when Brooks was trying to find out where you might have gone and Sheriff Fogel wasn't available because of some emergency at the Sacramento Airport, which I knew was about you, but no one believed me. Brooks apologized later, but Tom never did. On top of that, Beau was gone off somewhere and hadn't bothered to tell us where, just called and left a message."

"Yeah, well, he walked right into the spider's web. Didn't even know he was a hostage until I showed up. I swear guys are dense sometimes. Feed them chips and beer and give them either sports to watch or a project to work on, and they won't even come up for air until the world's already come to an end."

"They can't help it. It's the way they're put together. You've got to admit it has advantages. By the time they even realize something's wrong, the world's been saved, the emergency is over, and all they have to do is say phew, boy, that was a close one, and do a bunch of chest butts."

"Who came up with the whole chest butting thing anyway? That's got to be painful."

"Proves their manliness."

"What proves our manliness?" Jeremy, Meg's sixteen-year-old son, was standing in the doorway.

"Chest butts," I said.

"Chest butts? Bree, it's chest bumps, not chest butts, and it's about releasing adrenaline, not manliness. Why are you guys talking about chest bumps?"

"We're thinking of taking it up," I said.

"Yeah, right. You know what really proves our manliness?"

We shook our heads.

"Shaved heads. Makes guys look like giant dicks. Can't get more manly than that." Jeremy laughed at us and turned away, clumping up the stairs.

"What's got into him?" I asked Meg. "He never used to say stuff like that."

"He's on the varsity basketball team. Apparently, they all talk like that. His dad says he's going to crack down on him, but he won't. I think he's secretly pleased that Jer's growing up. It's pathetic."

"So what's been happening around here? Anyone dump their truck in the river?"

"Nah, everybody's been concentrating on finding you. And when we discovered you were in California, about ten people volunteered to go help find you. Tom sent Steve, and the rest of us chewed our nails and ate too many donuts while we waited for you to show up."

"Hey, I forgot to tell you. Shirl proposed to Steve Leftsky, and he accepted immediately. Smart guy. They're going to get married in May."

"No kidding. It's about time."

A day later I was in the office catching up on official reporter duties, which meant I was trying to figure out what to write about next. It was the hardest part of my job, searching the Internet for items of interest because not a thing was happening in town.

The door banged open, and Meg waltzed in.

"Beau's downstairs in the coffee shop, and he wants to talk to you." She was using the singsong voice she used when she was teasing me about men. I waited for her to start in on the whole he loves you, he wants your baby routine. When she didn't, I shrugged and went down to the coffee shop.

He was sitting in a booth at the back, which I thought was kind of unusual. It was easier to sit at the front of the coffee shop when your leg was in a cast. I sat on the bench across from him, ready for some heavy duty flirting, but the look on his face stopped me.

"Okay, spit it out." I tried to ignore the stone that had materialized in my stomach.

"I come home hoping for some peace while my leg is healing, and what happens? You get caught up in the dead woman thing again."

"I didn't do it on purpose"

"I don't want to spend my life worrying about what's happening to you. I can't do this, Bree. I thought I could, but I can't."

"Can't what? What are you saying exactly?"

"I can't spend all my time worrying what I'll find next time I see you. It's not any better when we're together, because then I'm worrying about what's going to happen to me, too. Shit, those days in California when I was a hostage and didn't know it were the most relaxing I've had since Jim dumped you. Not that I want you to go back to him. Actually, it would work better for me if you just stayed single."

"It works better for you if I just stay single?" I was getting dumped again. No surprise. Well, a little surprise. I cast back through my previous dumpings. I was pretty sure this wasn't the first time someone had wanted me to stay single. Men didn't want to be with me, but they didn't want anyone else to be with me either.

"If you're single, then I don't have to deal with my jealousy. I won't be tempted to try and win you back. If you're with someone, I have to stifle my urge to kill the bastard and take you back. It takes way less energy."

"You want me to stay single so you don't have to stop yourself from killing the guy I'm dating, but you don't want to stay with me because you'll have to worry too much?" My mind was reeling with the logic of it all, or maybe that was the lack of logic.

"Pretty much."

"In other words your inability to deal with your emotions is my fault, and if I just lived right, you'd be okay? Is that what you're saying?" Anger was starting to burn in my chest.

"I wouldn't put it quite like that. I just prefer the quiet life. You are the antithesis of that. Trouble follows you around like a dog."

"Speaking of dogs, what about Beans? What are you going to do with him?"

"Keep him. He can still come and stay with you when I'm away."

"You're dumping me and asking me to continue to take care of your dog? Why am I not surprised?"

I sat with my feet propped on the bench across from me, taking it all in and recapping in my mind. It was the same every time. I don't want to be with you anymore, but

I still want you to do me favors. Yep, that was the usual story.

"I can't make you want to be with me, but don't ask me to take care of your dog. He's your responsibility. If you didn't want to take care of him, you shouldn't have adopted him."

"I took him because I knew you wanted him. I did it for you. Anyway, he's old enough now that Tank won't eat him. He can be your dog."

"I don't want another dog." I almost added I couldn't afford another dog, but that would be ridiculous. It couldn't cost more than a five spot a month to keep that dog happy. Anyway, this wasn't a fight about the dog.

"You always want another dog. I understood when you were afraid Tank was going to eat him, but now? I think we've established that Beans has mastered Tank."

"Will you leave the dog out of it already? This is not about the dog. It's about you dumping me for the quiet life. Last I knew I was the one person you'd been waiting for your whole life. I'm having a hard time believing that you are letting that go because of a couple of freak incidents."

"But I am, MacGowan. I can't stand living with a pain in my stomach all the time. I can't do my best work if I'm always trying to keep track of where you are. You know why I didn't tell anyone I was going to California? I just wanted a few days' peace. No news of your latest body. No fires, no floods. Just peace. Not a battle to the death in the back of a moving Jeep."

I nodded and got up. What could I say to that? A battle to the death in the back of a moving Jeep. I went back to work.

Spring was finally threatening to arrive in Vermont. Snow persisted in the shadows and hollows, and my road was a mud hole; but the sun, when it appeared, was warm, and there was the smell of spring on the wind. There had been a media blitz when Senator Wallace disappeared, but after that died down, there hadn't been any news or sightings of him. The excitement in South Royalton was Steve and Shirl's upcoming wedding.

Bets were being swapped at the local bar. A third of the community's members were willing to put good money on the wedding being a non-starter. If Steve was smart, he wouldn't show. There was a lot of good-natured bickering over their chances of staying married, and Meg had asked me to do an article on the failure rate of peace officers' marriages.

I was doing internet research. It was kind of depressing. The sound of the dogs barking interrupted my train of thought.

"Shut up! I'm working in here!" I shouted. I figured they could hear me even though the door was closed. The barking didn't stop. If anything, it got louder and more frantic. Not good. I got up to see what animal they had cornered. It wouldn't be the first time I had to call the dogs into the house so a poor raccoon they had treed could escape.

I knew the moment I opened the door that it wasn't a raccoon. The odor smacked me in the face and made my eyes run. Great. I opened the kennels I kept on the porch for occasions like this and called the dogs. Ranger and Hank bounded up the stairs, tails going a mile a minute, their goofy faces all pleased with themselves. They reeked. My eyes stung, and I had to stifle a desire to puke.

"Annie! Diesel! Get you butts up here! Now!"

Diesel came first trotting sideways, torn between obeying his mom and the marvelous toy he'd been playing with. Annie came last, head down, tail between her legs. She knew she'd been bad. I about died when they got close. If anything, they smelled worse than Hank and Ranger. Ho, boy.

I went in search of peroxide, but there wasn't any in the house. The dogs would just have to stink until morning.

I sat back down at the keyboard and tried to concentrate on my article. I really needed to show Meg some progress, but before I hit a single key Annie was sounding again, not her normal bark, but the deep baying of a hound dog. Puzzled, I looked out the window in the porch door. That stinking skunk had come right up onto the porch and was attempting to pull Annie's bed out from under her between the bars of the crate.

"What the …" I turned on the porch light and banged on the door, but the skunk ignored me. 1850s farmhouses are not generally airtight, and the smell coming under the door was making my nose burn. The lights were on, the dogs were going absolutely nuts, I was banging on the door, and that stupid skunk was trying to steal Annie's bed. I had to tell Meg about this.

"Rabid," she said. "It's got to be rabid. You need to call the game warden."

"It's gone now. I'll call the warden, but I don't think he's going to want to search for it."

"Everything else OK? Do you know when Beau's coming home?"

"No, last I heard – oh, my God! That little bugger is back again. He just backed up to Diesel's crate and sprayed him again. I'll call you back. The smell is awful."

I hung up the phone and dropped it on the kitchen table. How was I going to lure that sucker off my porch? I grabbed a can of Annabelle's cat food and popped the lid. Slipping out of the door on the other side of the house I skirted around until I was in the drive on the porch side. I waved the can around in the air hoping that the smell would attract the skunk, then I set the can on the ground, ran back around the house and into the kitchen.

Picking up the phone, I dialed Max as I went to look out the window. The skunk was still poking his nose into the kennels, taunting the dogs, but he must have caught the scent of the cat food because he lifted his nose in the air and sniffed. He was ambling down the stairs as Max answered his phone.

"Max!" I interrupted his greeting. "Grab your .22 and get down here. I've got this weird skunk tormenting my dogs."

"Why don't you shoot him yourself? You used to do target practice with your brothers."

"I don't have any guns down here. I got rid of them when Meg started having kids. Oh, just get down here, will you?"

I hung up the phone. I was antsy, jiggling my leg and hoping Max would get here before the skunk took off. I really didn't want my dogs bitten by a crazy, rabid Pepé Le Pew from hell. The skunk finished his food and wandered off toward the chicken house. I wasn't worried about the chickens; the coop was critter proof as long as the gate was shut, which I knew it was.

Max arrived in time to see our stinky friend disappear into the weeds behind the house. He took a shot at the creature, but I don't think he hit it.

"Shoot!" I wasn't mad at Max as much as I was disappointed we hadn't gotten rid of the skunk.

"I can't shoot, Bree. Can't hit what I can't see. Sorry it took me so long. I had to put on my pants."

"No, I didn't mean for you to *shoot*, I meant shoot like *dang*, dang, that stupid skunk got away. That's all. I appreciate you coming down here, though."

"Well, call me if he comes back again." Max headed back up the road, .22 over his shoulder.

It seemed smarter to go in the back way, even though the skunk was gone. No point in dragging more stink into the house than necessary. The phone was ringing when I walked in. I hurried to pick it up.

"So what happened?" Meg's voice was excited.

"Boy, you'd think I was going to win the lottery from the sound of you. Nothing happened. I lured the skunk off the porch with a can of cat food, which it proceeded to eat before Max got down here. Now it'll come back thinking it'll get more tuna or something. I'd hate skunks if they weren't so damn funny." Truthfully, I found it hard to hate many things except Lucy Howe. She was a sneaky little back stabber, and she deserved to be hated. Now she was a real skunk.

When I came downstairs the next morning, the skunk was curled up on the top of Annie's crate. I found my cell phone and snapped a picture, since no one would believe me if I didn't have a picture. I popped the tops on a couple of cans of cat food and went outside in my pajamas. Walking around to the kitchen porch, I dropped a trail of cat food from my house down the road to a spot where an unused run-off pipe ran under the road. I set the can in the ditch next to the culvert and backed away. I was hoping that the radio fence would keep the dogs from the skunk, and the proximity to a good sleeping place would keep the skunk away from the house. I trotted back up the road hoping no one would drive by and see me in my jammies. Not that they were indecent, a pair of sweat shorts and a T-shirt, but I didn't need any more talk than usual about me in town.

The skunk and I got into a routine. I fed him morning and evening, he stayed away from the house. We had a deal. I was satisfied with the arrangement. Tom offered to kill the thing, but I declined. The thing was now named Stripes. Meg thought I was crazy, and Tom just shook his head at me, but I was okay with it. It saved me from killing a fellow creature and kept the stink out of the house.

The day of Steve's wedding, I was out of cat food. I ran a little dry dog food down the road to the culvert and hoped that satisfied Stripes for the time being. Then I went upstairs and stood in front of my closet door, the usual dilemma staring me in the face. I didn't know what to wear. The black dress I bought in California was cute, but I was afraid to wear black to a wedding. Black was a funeral color. So I pulled out an almost modest red dress and the black shoes from California. Then I drove down the hill into town to get my hair done.

The owner of Planet Hair can do hair like no one I've ever met. It's always perfect, and while I can't ever make it look quite that good again, when I want to look good,

Denise is who I go and see. She also has her finger on the pulse of the Upper Valley, so if you're feeling out of touch, an hour in her salon will take care of that too.

"Tell me again why you didn't call your salon Locks and Gossip?" I teased her as she shampooed my hair.

"Oh, stop." She rinsed the suds out of my hair and sat me up with a towel around my head. "Hey, did those guys who were looking for you ever find you?"

"What guys? Were they good looking?"

"The first one was too old for you. Came in yesterday asking about you. I told him I didn't know where you lived. I offered your work phone, but he wasn't interested. The second came in this morning. Wanted to know if you'd be going to the wedding. Strange. Didn't know you were so popular with the men."

I snorted.

"I'm not. Probably bill collectors," but I didn't believe that. Unease began to grow in my stomach again.

"I wouldn't worry too much about them. You could take them if it came to a fight."

"Very funny, Denise."

That afternoon Max picked me up and took me to town for the wedding. There was no point in everyone on the hill driving down to the church, and if we wanted to come home in separate vehicles, there would be plenty of rides to choose from.

Outside the church Miles was straightening Tom's bow tie in front of a short line of men with ties hanging. A chorus of smiles and greetings came from the group as I approached Miles.

"Hey, Bree, I'm in the middle of something. Do you mind seating yourself?"

"Sure. Where's Steve? Shouldn't he be hanging out with you guys?"

"He's in the men's room thinking about tossing his cookies," Tom said.

"At least he's only thinking about it." I smiled at the guys and pushed through the red doors.

The last time I had been in this church was for Vera's funeral. I felt my mood dropping as the memories of the day flooded in on me. *Forget it*, I told myself. This is a happy day. I deliberately walked past the rear church pew that I'd sat in on that day and made my way to the front. Shirl had picked up on the dancing down the aisle rage, and I wanted to be able to see the whole thing.

Meg crashed through the door with her brood. Gemma and Pete ran down the church and into my pew for hugs. Sara and Jeremy sat behind me and leaned their forearms on the seat back. Sara whispered to Jeremy as a large woman in a very short skirt sat across the aisle from us. They burst into giggles, and Meg gave them what could only be called the beady eyeball.

"Easy you two," I said. "Remember, adults can have their feelings hurt, too."

Jeremy had the grace to look ashamed of himself, but Sara just grinned at me.

"She must have a lot of self-confidence to wear that to church, Bree. I don't think I have to worry about hurting her feelings."

The church filled quickly, and it wasn't long before strains of music filled the room. A low mutter followed. Instead of traditional wedding music, Hawaiian ukulele strumming filled the hall. Before I had a chance to wonder at Shirl's choice of music, the first of the bridesmaids

started down the aisle. She was dressed in a grass skirt and
bikini top. Her feet were bare, and wrapped around her
ankles and wrists were strands of ... seaweed? I bit my
bottom lip to keep from grinning. A second and third
attendant followed the first. They were dressed identically,
but the effect was rather different on each of them.

"Oh my gosh, Bree, do you believe this?" Sara's voice
was quiet in my ear. "The first one looks OK, but they
should have stuffed that one girl's bra. I can't say what I'm
thinking about the last one."

Sara had a point. The third girl was truly magnificent.
The cups of her bikini barely contained her breasts, and
her belly was big and round as well. As she danced her
body undulated in a hypnotic sway that made me wonder
if we were going to end up seeing more of her than we
maybe cared to.

I glanced around at the guests sitting in the pews. Shell
shock was the word that came to mind. Several people had
their mouths hanging open, and there were a couple of
faces so red that I was worried someone would have heart
failure. Steve and Tom had huge grins on their faces. They
had known what was coming, and they were enjoying it to
the fullest.

"Where do you suppose they got the seaweed?" I
whispered to Sara.

"Iparty," she whispered back. "They have this whole
section for luaus."

Meg shot me a dirty look and shushed Sara.

Meg's whisper died away as Shirl appeared at the back
of the church. I'd never seen anything quite like her get-
up. Her hair was braided on top of her head, and she wore
a veil and white pearls. Her bikini top was white satin and

lace. Instead of a grass skirt, she wore an ankle length satin skirt layered with strips of torn white lace. The effect could have been very sea-weedy, if the skirt had been green. It was simply bizarre. Her feet were bare like those of her bridesmaids, only she had strips of lace hanging from her ankles and wrists.

Shirl minced the tiny steps of the hula while waving her hands in an intricate pattern. If we'd been mesmerized by the bridesmaids, now we were hypnotized. Each step brought her about four inches closer to the altar. The elaborate motions of her hands told a story. The only problem was I didn't think any of us had a clue what they were supposed to be saying. Presumably, it was a song of love and devotion, but who knew? It could have been the story of John and Yoko. I'd never know the difference.

I glanced to where Steve was waiting with Tom. They both still wore oversized grins. I glanced back to Shirl. She had her bottom lip pulled under her top teeth and the corners of her mouth were twitching, and I realized she was trying not to laugh. Instead of wedding nerves, Steve and Shirl were having fun.

I recognized the feeling in the pit of my stomach as jealousy. I wanted what they had. Hell, I wanted a relationship that lasted more than a few months. I could already imagine what the Leftsky kids would look like. Blonde hair, blue eyes, devilish grins. They'd be the happiest kids in Vermont. Shirl would have everything I'd ever wanted, not that I'd ever wanted more than friendship with Steve. At least there was one guy in the area I could say I'd never thought about dating. Steve and I were friends, good friends.

The feeling that I was missing something persisted through the ceremony. As the minister made the usual introduction of the newly married couple, I considered skipping the reception. No point in taking my sulky face to a party. I was looking for the best way to escape the crowd at the front of the church when Miles joined me.

"You have to come to the reception, you know. You're Steve's oldest friend. Actually, I'm kind of surprised he didn't ask you to be the best man."

"Very funny. Do I have to go to the reception? I'm really not in the mood."

"You're just feeling self-conscious because you don't have a date. Why don't you ride over with me? That way, you can sit with me."

"I thought you were with the wedding party."

"Nah, I'm just an usher. Tom's the best man. Come on."

Miles grabbed my arm and pulled me over to his truck. "Get in."

I was just about to jump in when I remembered the cat food.

"You go on ahead. I've got to get some cat food, or Stripes will start spraying the house again."

"You've got a cat named Stripes?"

"No, a skunk. It's a long story, and I'll tell it to you at the reception. If I get cat food now, I can put it in Max's truck, and he'll drop it at the house for me."

I trotted across the green and into the little market. It took me less than three minutes to grab the cat food and pay. The truck was where we left it before the wedding, so I dropped the cat food on the seat and went looking for Max. I stepped between two cars parked on the street and waited for a car to pass before I crossed, but instead of going by, it slowed, then stopped in front of me. Before I figured out who was in it, the window slid down, and I could see a gun pointing directly at my heart.

"Get in the car."

It was Wallace. So the senator wasn't in Mexico. His voice was as smooth as when he was trying to convince me to accuse innocent men of murder. Well, maybe not innocent, but not guilty of killing his wife. The gun shook in his hand. I opened the door and got in before I ended up with an extra hole in my body.

When Senator Wallace drove into my drive, Stripes was standing on the edge of the yard waiting for dinner. Wallace gunned the engine and aimed for the skunk.

"No!" I lurched sideways and shoved Wallace's arm to the left. The car swerved, and I couldn't tell if Stripes had been hit, but I didn't smell the telltale odor that accompanied the death of a skunk. Wallace slammed on the brakes, and I darted out of the car and up the front steps. Stripes was also moving toward the house on a collision course with the dogs who had come tearing around the back of the house, barking like mad.

"Annie, no! Go back!" But Annie was having no part of it. She raced past Stripes and up the steps to jump on me. Ranger and Hank ignored the skunk as well, but Diesel had to stop for a sniff. I rushed to open the door and herd the other dogs into the kitchen before Stripes blasted him. I slammed and locked the door. Horrified, I watched as the dog touched noses with the skunk, but nothing happened. They stood there nose to nose, Diesel's hind end going like crazy. I swear Stripes lifted his head and kissed the dog.

That's when the senator, who had finally extracted himself from the car, came storming up the walk. As he reached the animals, Diesel turned and growled, the hair along his back standing up in a brindle Mohawk. Wallace bent his knee and kicked Diesel hard under his jaw. Diesel yelped and made for the house, his tail between his legs.

I opened the door to let Diesel in, and as I slammed it shut I heard the senator yell. I looked out to see Stripes, tail high, back end in the air, giving the man all he had. Wallace stood frozen, hands over his mouth, absolute disgust in his eyes, which were running with tears like there was no tomorrow.

"That's it!" he yelled. "I'm taking care of this once and for all!" He kicked out at Stripes, who trotted out of range, and stomped over to the car. He had a gun in his hand when he turned back to the house. "I'm going to pop a cap up your fucking ass!" His voice was so high that my ears hurt listening to him. He pointed the gun in the direction of the retreating skunk and fired off a couple of rounds.

He turned toward the house, looked directly in my eyes, and brought the gun up. I dropped to the ground and crawled away. The first shot shattered the window in the kitchen door, sending glass flying everywhere. I called the dogs to me, and we scrambled across the kitchen floor as bullets thudded into the house.

I sat at the bottom of the stairs, my back to the wall, hugging the dogs to me. My heart was beating so fast I couldn't get enough air. The shooting had stopped. I expected Wallace to burst through the door at any moment. Bile was rising into my throat. Nothing happened. I strained my ears but I couldn't hear anything. I let go of the dogs and got up. I crept up the stairs and sneaked down the hall to the bedroom overlooking the porch.

Wallace had the trunk of his rental car open and was rifling through the contents. I didn't know what he was searching for, but I was really hoping it wasn't explosives. I dug my cell phone out of my pocket and called Tom at the barracks. The State Police may not be near enough for the troopers to get here before Wallace left, but maybe they would catch him on the road.

Whatever it was he was looking for, he didn't find it. He let out a yell of pure frustration and threw his gun at my house. It thudded against the wall. Wallace took a couple of deep breaths and, having calmed himself, got in the car and drove away.

My knees shook as I stumbled back down the stairs. I knelt down to look at Diesel. I slid my hands along and under his jaw. He didn't flinch, and there didn't appear to be any serious injury, but the next call I made was to my vet. That idiot Wallace was going to be easy to catch.

Tom caught up with me at the veterinarian's office. Diesel had been x-rayed and found to be sound. He was fussed over by the doctor and vet's assistants when they heard what had happened. When Tom came in, he had a huge grin on his face, and I smiled in return.

"Did they get him?"

"Just like you thought. He took his rental back to the airport stinking to high heaven. The rental agency called the New Hampshire State Police. They caught up with him arguing with the gate attendant at SWA. They weren't going to let him on board reeking of skunk regardless of what state he was senator of."

"What'll happen to him?"

"I imagine he'll be extradited to California. After he serves that sentence, he can come back here and serve time for attempted murder."

"That would be good." I gave Tom a hug and loaded Diesel in the truck.

A wave of sadness hit me as I pulled into my drive. My house was a mess. The sadness faded, and an intense desire to hurt Senator Wallace hit me. He had ruined my home. I surveyed the damage. Well, maybe it wasn't trashed. The kitchen door would have to be replaced along with some pieces of siding, but other than that, it was still the same old house.

I got out of the car, let Diesel out and walked over to the gun still lying in my flowerbed, the instrument of Stripe's demise. Proud of myself for remembering not to just pick the thing up, I went onto the porch to find a rag or towel. There's always stuff like that lying around. Not that I'm a slob, but the dogs love to drag stuff out of the house.

I went to pull an old towel out of Tank's bed, and there, curled into a ball, was Stripes without a scratch to be seen. He lifted his head and looked at me reproachfully. I hadn't fed him his dinner. I ran to the truck and pulled out the forgotten cans of cat food from where Max had left them and popped one open. Everything else in my life might be shit, but my hungry skunk was still alive.

I left the open can of cat food on the floor and turned back to the house. I pushed open the door and stopped on the threshold. The glass had been swept from the floor. The chair I had toppled scurrying away from the door had been righted, and there on the table was a large dress box topped with a bow.

"Hello?" I called. "Anybody here?"

There wasn't an answering call, and the dogs were looking at me like I was crazy, so I figured we must be alone. No way my dogs would ignore an extra body in the house. They'd be hunting them down for either love or lunch.

I tore the ribbon from the box and opened it. On top of the tissue paper was a small piece of notepaper folded in half. I lifted it up and unfolded it.

*I thought you might like to have these.*

That's all. No signature. No "hope you are okay," nothing.

I folded back the tissue paper and there, freshly clean and neatly folded, rested the blue dress and the matching blue shoes.

# Meet Author Kate George

Ms. George has enjoyed a life-long love affair with mysteries, and by age 25 had written her first book, a truly awful novella. She then wisely took a break from writing. When Ms. George realized that she could use her own off-beat sense of humor in her work, she began writing seriously again. Ms George loves animals and they find their way into her writing. The incident with the crazy skunk in *California Schemin'* (March 2011) is a true account. For the record, the dogs would rather stink than be washed with peroxide, baking soda or dishwashing soap ever again.

CPSIA information can be obtained at www.ICGtesting.com
Printed in the USA
LVOW070001161211

259558LV00001B/48/P